Saint Theresa

and

Sleeping with Strangers

Saint Theresa
and
Sleeping with Strangers

Bahaa Abdelmegid

❖

Translated by
Chip Rossetti

The American University in Cairo Press
Cairo   New York

First published in 2010 by
The American University in Cairo Press
113 Sharia Kasr el Aini, Cairo, Egypt
420 Fifth Avenue, New York, NY 10018
www.aucpress.com

Dar el Kutub No. 13821/09
ISBN 978 977 416 340 1

Dar el Kutub Cataloging-in-Publication Data

Abdelmegid, Bahaa
        Saint Theresa and Sleeping with Strangers / Bahaa Abdelmegid;
    translated by Chip Rossetti.—Cairo: The American University in Cairo
    Press, 2009
        p.   cm.
        ISBN 978 977 416 340 1
        1. Arabic fiction   II. Title
        892.73

1 2 3 4 5 6 7 8   14 13 12 11 10

Designed by Sebastian Schönenstein
Printed in Egypt

Saint Theresa

To her who was the world to me, and then . . .

To my mother, in hope of eternal life

The Spirit is Willing but the Flesh is Weak

Sorrowful Blue Glass

At the same moment that Budur opened her eyes, there was a very pregnant mouse looking for a place to bear its young. Perhaps it was looking for some dry crusts of bread to nibble on, while saving a piece for the litter on its way.

Budur looked around her and found her sisters pressed up against her on both sides of the mattress. She gently moved aside the legs of one and sluggishly propped herself up, trying to make her way across their bodies. The image of the Virgin was directly in front of her, and Budur silently invoked her name. She entered the bathroom, washed her face, and wiped away the traces of dreams, chasing away the phantoms and fears within her. A brief flash from a dream came back to her—she was sinking in a river, surrounded by fish that were eating her body. As she struggled to ascend into the sunlight, whose rays reached down to the air bubbles she was breathing out, she saw a wooden cross covered in

5

green algae. She tried to grab it to save herself from sinking further, but when she grasped it, it dissolved between her fingers and she dropped to the bottom. Soon she was sinking deeper and deeper into the muddy silt.

She opened the window of the room that looked down on the alley. Through the window she saw her neighbor Sawsan fixing her hair in the mirror, as the voice of Shaykh Muhammad Refaat flowed over the air, softly intoning eloquent verses from the Holy Qur'an. Budur said good morning to her, then entered the main room. There she met her mother, who reminded her that she had to finish cleaning the house quickly, because the two of them would be going to the Church of Saint Theresa that morning.

She was used to going to Saint Theresa's every Sunday with her mother. They would bring along bread for the poor that her mother, despite their own poverty, insisted on making every week. Her mother felt satisfaction whenever she saw the looks of gratitude in the eyes of the needy, and she thanked God that she was better off than they were. She remembered what Christ Our Lord had said, "If someone takes your cloak, do not stop him from taking your tunic." But whenever Budur's mother thought about the future, she felt anxiety and fear: what would she do in this world by herself? She had been widowed young, and her husband had left her with three daughters, Budur being the oldest. She herself had grown up in a humble village beside Lake Qarun. The people there had made a living by fishing, and so it was known as Fishermen's Village. How many years had she spent gazing on the lake, with its mud-brown waters that turn blood red as soon as the sun begins to set? When the night departed with its worries and stars, her grandfather would go out to the lake and bring back shimmering fish, just as Christ's apostles had done. Her heart leaped in her throat when she saw the fish struggling, as they tried to escape from the nets, and she wept for them. That same day, her grandfather went down to the lake, saying, "I am going to look for Qarun's treasure, lost under the waters. God drowned Qarun, his palace, and everything he owned to punish him for his arrogance and his failure to show his family and clan the proper respect." As for her uncle, he plunged into the water, saying, "I am going to fetch the elixir of life that Qarun used to turn dust into gold!" Her grandfather drowned, and her uncle never resurfaced.

The rumor spread in the village that their family was cursed, and that Budur's grandmother would have to enter the ruins of Qarun's palace and ask permission of the jinn and devils that dwelled there to lift this affliction from her and her family. Her grandmother returned from the ruins a different person. She took to climbing onto the roof of the house, talking to the moon at night and to the sun at midday. Sometimes she would run toward the moonlight reflected on the waters of the lake, claiming she could hear the voices of her ancestors. They were coming up from the depths to the lakeshore, now that they had completed their allotted punishment.

When she was asked, "Where are they?" she replied, "They will not appear to you until they renounce the faith of the Jews and become Christian!"

She began to offer them food—eggs, lettuce, and salted fish—that she would set out on the lakeshore. She would let down her hair and tell them, "Come to heaven's table, come to Christ's table!"

"The woman is mad," said the people of the village. "Expel her from this town, or she'll bring down Qarun's curse on us all." Budur's family decided to head west to Libya, but the grandmother said they should walk in the direction of the pyramid that she could see from her balcony. So they set out, walking parallel to the Nile, until they reached Shubra. Then she said, "Let us rest here, and build ourselves a shack."

No sooner had they finished building the shack than the grandmother gave up the ghost. On her chest they placed a cross and a star that she used to keep in her brassiere. Then, when devils burned down the shack one night, they moved somewhere else. Next to what was left of the shack, Budur's mother placed a cross she made out of fishbones. Soon thereafter, Budur's father, Hafez, found a humble room beside the Church of Saint Theresa. "Grandmother's ghost won't be able to reach this place," he said, "the Virgin will protect us."

He didn't know what kind of work he would do in Shubra, or how he would feed his children. When he told his story to the church priest, the priest told him, "Take up fishing—there is a blessing in it." Hafez was afraid of the Nile: ever since his father had died in the lake, he was frightened of murky waters. He ended up choking to death on a fishbone that caught in his throat.

When he departed this world, he left behind nothing but five ratls of fish in a basket that sat beside the door to the one-room apartment. Budur's mother Linda was obliged to help clean the church in return for puny wages. Linda's brother Iwad used to offer them assistance from time to time. They lived together in the same neighborhood and tried to forget all about the grandmother and the lake. They said, "If we want to live, we must bury the dead, and put the past behind us for the time being." Budur grew up and kept the secret of Qarun's palace and the riddle of her grandmother's madness. She never told anyone, and no one dared ask her. The neighborhood near the church and the al-Khazandar Mosque grew crowded with people. The greenery, trees, and farmlands disappeared, and all that remained of the canal was the name of a public street packed on both sides with humble houses and tall apartment buildings. Because they were poor, her family's home remained as it was. Budur never finished her education, and left school after getting her middle-school diploma. But she still loved reading newspapers and the occasional short story. Sometimes she read the Bible within earshot of her kindly neighbor, Said's mother, who used to lean her head out to hear her, as if she could understand what was being read aloud, and remark, "Every word from our Lord is good."

Budur's voice was beautiful, and her face light-skinned. Her eyes were green, and when she walked down the street, eyes followed her, staring at her bosom and legs. One of her neighbors followed her one night. He climbed the stairs behind her, and tried to kiss her. She resisted, but she still remembered his kiss and wished on several occasions that someone would rush at her with the same daring as Said did—Said, who had been a soldier in the '67 War and didn't return. "He died a martyr," they said. "He is a

9

prisoner," they said. Whenever she heard his name she remembered his kiss.

At Easter, her uncle Iwad visited them. Her mother's heart leaped between her ribs when her brother brought her the good news that there was a suitor for Budur who wished to wed her in holy matrimony. She hadn't thought that Budur would be able to get married in these days following the Naksa, as they called the '67 defeat.

They didn't put on a big wedding, out of respect for the feelings of their neighbor, Said's mother, whose son was gone. He had left her and his sister Sawsan on their own.

Girgis

Girgis came on Sunday, just before five o'clock. He had wanted to get there early, fearing that an attack might happen during his visit to Budur. He had no desire to be an omen of misfortune just as he was starting to get to know her. He had never laid eyes on her, but he had heard about her from his sisters who used to see her in church, and who praised her beautiful voice, since she sang hymns with the choir.

Now he worked as a tailor in a shop downtown. At the beginning of his working life, he had worked in the Gattinio Building. Then, based on a recommendation from the owner of the big shop, he switched to working for the khawaga Luka with a salary of twenty pounds plus tips. He was thirty years old, and was thinking seriously about marriage. He had come to hate his sinning, and wanted to repent after almost getting himself killed the previous Saturday when he went to his sweetheart's place in Imbaba. He had knocked on the door, and she greeted him with

10

kisses. Then they lay down together, naked, on the floor. That was the last thing he remembered, until he found himself at the bottom of the staircase covered in blood. Some passersby recognized him and took him to the hospital. He praised God that he was all right, and the others had kept silent about the incident, for fear of public disgrace.

Budur, with her beautiful face and trim outfit, appeared before him. She was carrying a tray with cups of tea on it. She set it down, her hands trembling lightly, and sat beside her mother. On the other side sat her uncle Iwad, who broke the silence by declaring that Girgis wanted to marry Budur. Girgis was a broad-shouldered man, with a wide chest. Some hair peeked out over his neck and chest. His hands were strong, his voice soft. She asked herself, *Does he like singing? I will sing for him when we are by ourselves at home.*

They finished the meeting by setting the date for the wedding ceremony. Her mother was very happy, because Budur wouldn't be far from her: there was a room available in the same alley. She would give it a nice coat of paint and furnish it with the best furnishings, and everything would be for the best.

Sawsan

The day of Budur's wedding wasn't the first time I went to the church. Sometimes when I was little I would sneak over to it to pick the flowers. The guard would notice me, but he didn't scold me, or run after me. I would see the children on Friday returning from church carrying in their hands beautiful colored portraits of the Virgin and Child. My brother Said scolded me when he found me holding one of these images. I became jealous of them and wondered, *Why don't we Muslims have pictures too?*

The night of the wedding the church was packed. With Girgis, she approached the altar, wearing a white dress. Shy. The priest appeared and chanted some hymns, and told Girgis and Budur, "You are one body." The bells began to ring, and the deacons surrounded them with quiet chanting. The scent of incense clung to the air in the church. There were smiling faces, men and women mingled, and the children made a ruckus. I noticed my mother at a distance: she had cast off her mourning clothes and there was a smile on her face. Maybe she was thinking about a marriage for me, or maybe she was recalling for a moment her own wedding, and the joy of discovering she had become a woman. She was engrossed in conversation with her neighbors; laughter rang out in all directions and reverberated in the church's dome.

From time to time, my mother and I go to Saint Theresa. The silence that envelops the place terrifies me, with its images of saints looking up to heaven as they raise their hands in a gesture of peace. I see an image of Him as an infant surrounded by a halo of light. And His immaculate mother looks at Him affectionately with her radiant, angelic face. The sunbeams that pierce the stained-glass windows and the brown wooden pews induce me to sit down on them. I look at the cross over the altar, and I see Him on it, with His arms spread and His head bowed, although His eyes are looking up to heaven. His head is covered with a crown of thorns. His gaze flooded with sorrow used to astonish and sadden me. I want to go up to Him, bring Him down and give Him water to drink. I want to bandage His wounds for Him; I want to remove His crown of thorns and replace it with a garland of jasmine and gold. Without looking at it herself, my mother orders me out, saying, "You will go mad." She pulls me away by my warm hands, and we pass between the marble bowls of holy water. I leave her and sneak off to the sepulcher of Saint Theresa, overcome by a desire to enter this glass coffin. I lie down and stretch out my weary body. I can feel the coldness of the place: I'm breaking its silence with my presence.

We leave the church and ride the Sayyida Zeinab tram from the stop at the al-Khazandar Mosque, where I used to go to memorize the Qur'an at the feet of a shaykh who lived across the street from it. He would always say, "The Qur'an is a light unto you, on earth and in heaven." We would get off when the conductor called out, "Umm Hashim!" and in front of the tomb we would relieve ourselves of our basket of sprouted fuul. As soon as someone noticed what we were doing, we would find ourselves surrounded by a large group of poor people and beggars. Inevitably, the basket would be empty in the blink of an eye. As the sweat poured from her forehead my mother would try in a hoarse voice to ask them to pray for my brother Said to return to his mother safe and sound. Some of them would pray, but the rest would be busy gobbling down the food. After the afternoon prayer, we would exit the tomb area just as the custodian was saying, "No women after five o'clock!" and then leave the shrine. I could still smell the scent of rosewater on the palms of my hands after I brushed them on the tomb's silver-coated railing, imitating what my mother and other people did.

Conditions in our alley have grown worse because of the war, and most of the time the houses are dark. An attack comes and we hear voices calling to put out the fires. We hurry to the basements, or flee to the few available shelters. We children keep fear from slipping into us by making noise and yelling. With enthusiastic voices, we shriek:

> Hey Aziz! Hey Aziz!
> A plague on the English, if you please!

Sometimes I find pens and coins on the ground. Once I picked up a pen from beneath my foot and I wanted to write a letter to my brother and tell him that I was scared, that the attacks and the war frighten me and freeze my veins. Stretchers carrying the dead pass by our streets and their mothers' wails terrify me. Nightmares haunt me in my sleep. I will tell him that I miss him, just like I miss my father and the feeling of being safe, since there is no tender hand to caress me, no man to protect me and keep my fears at bay. I will tell him, *I look up at the sky every night, and ask the one who raised the heavens to bring you back to me and my mother so we can feel like living again.* I will beg him and tell him, *Come back, Said, so that we can be happy, and I can feel safe because you're here with me.* When my mother saw the pen, she reprimanded me, saying, "You wanna die like those people at Bahr al-Baqar? You can't have it: we know what those people we're up against are capable of!" I was sad because I couldn't keep the pen, and I was even sadder because I didn't send the letter.

The neighbors say that the Jews killed my brother Said, but my brother wasn't killed, and we never got his body back. My brother didn't die: maybe he got lost on the way, maybe his leg was broken and he wasn't able to walk across the vast desert, which I visited on a school trip to the pyramids.

As enormous as those giant mounds are, I couldn't go all the way around the biggest one. I almost fell when one of my friends and I raced each other on top of one of the big stone piles. In the desert a foreign lady gave me an apple. Her face was red from the sun's heat and beads of sweat appeared on her forehead. I said hello to her and she spoke to me but I didn't understand her. I only remember the apple that was red like the color of blood, and the nice smell. I can still recall that smell whenever I see apples. The foreign lady disappeared in the desert like a grain of sand. Maybe she remembers me just like I remember her. Maybe she remembers the child whom she met, took a liking to, and gave an apple to. Maybe this is the woman who will come across Said and rescue him.

Luka

The khawaga Luka, the owner of the tailor shop, was of Jewish origin. He had come to Cairo from Greece a long time ago but didn't emigrate with those who went to Israel after the founding of that nation. He did not have an advanced education, but he spoke Arabic and English fluently. He wasn't an ordinary-looking man: he was handsome and the sun gave him a beautiful bronze color. He smiled a lot, and his fine black hair fell in long locks over his forehead. He was on the tall side, and had a physique that suggested regular exercise. He wasn't married and he was scrupulous about praying at the synagogue on Adli Street. Saturday was his private day when he retreated from daily life for the Sabbath and Girgis would come to him to prepare his food and then leave.

He was twelve when he arrived in Alexandria with his mother Sasha, after his father, who had been living there on his own, died. His mother had come to claim what remained of his father's business, but she only found debts. She traveled to Cairo and tried her luck at dancing and acting, but never fulfilled her dream of success, having instead fallen in love with a failed director. She soon realized that he wanted her for his own gratification—and for that of others. She was an alcoholic and suffered for years before regaining her self-confidence. She had brief flings with men who passed through her life, until she finally settled down with a taxi driver who loved her very much. He insisted that she leave the burlesque houses behind, and he supported her and her son. She hated for Luka to see her with a man other than his father, although the child had accepted the new situation without raising a fuss. But when he realized that the driver wanted to marry his mother, he heatedly objected and left the house. She ended the relationship in disgrace after the driver's wife came and accused her of being a homewrecker, declaring that western women cause nothing but trouble and their bodies are like public property. Some of Luka's mother's friends offered to loan her some money, so she rented a studio to cut clothes, which she had some experience in. With time she mastered the trade of tailoring and became well known in upper-class Egyptian circles. Her son was able to retain the shop's good reputation after his mother's death.

Luka usually went to Alexandria every Sunday morning and came back on the last train. At one of the birthday parties he was invited to there, he met an Italian woman named Sabina. They danced all night and he told her about his longing for a kindred soul who would understand him and could share his life in Cairo. They parted and agreed to meet again.

The relationship between them grew stronger. Each took an interest in the other's life. They would go to the beach, where she surrendered to his flirtations and kisses. He told her, "You have become an important part of my life," and asked her to marry him. Sabina was delighted by his embrace of her at that moment but she was caught off guard since she did not want to get married now and wasn't certain about her feelings toward him. Marriage was an eternal bond that only God could break. So she put off giving him an answer, thanks to the fact that the decision wasn't hers alone to make: there was her father whom she had to consult. "I'd like to get out of the water," she said. "I want to go; I've stayed too long."

"But you didn't tell me what you think! I want to hear your answer now."

"Not now. Let's not talk about it. I don't have an answer ready. I'll give you one soon."

Sabina's father gave his daughter the freedom to act as she wished in the affairs of her life. At first he did not forbid her from becoming friends with Luka, but because he was a devout Catholic, he felt that a Christian woman marrying a Jew was an impossibility. One Sunday evening while they were listening to the radio and sipping tea she asked him, "Do you want some dessert?"

"Thank you, no dessert. I'm trying to cut back on sugar, as you know."

"I know, I was just testing your willpower."

"You know well the extent of my willpower."

"And are you aiming that willpower of yours in my direction?"

"Not exactly, but I do want to see an end to that relationship."

"The end, as Luka proposed, is marriage."

"And what do you think about it?"

"Would that change your position?"

"Well, you know I am opposed to it."

"That's what I always expected."

"Have you been straightforward with him about it?"

"I didn't have a chance to explain: he was happy and optimistic. I didn't want to hurt his pride at the same moment he was asking me to share my life with him. I couldn't do something that I wouldn't want done to me."

Sabina's father was ready with his response, which he made as if he were making an important statement: "The Jews have no future! Their lives are constantly threatened, ever since Hitler declared war on them, when they were like mice hiding in ditches and underground. Of course Luka is a fine young man, but I don't want you and your children to end up in the gas chambers!"

"You are talking about a history that ended fifteen years ago: this is 1958! Luka doesn't want to go to Israel or anywhere else. He's become an Egyptian. Regardless of what you believe about his religion, I will try—maybe I'll even succeed—in making him Catholic."

"Sabina! My final word is that I do not consent! Luka is threatened by death at any time. Abd al-Nasser won't leave any Jew in Egypt, since he's at war now with the great powers.

18

Didn't England steal the Palestinians' land and give it to the Jews? Didn't Israel preside over attacks on Egypt in the War of '56? Didn't—"

"Father, can we drop the subject?" responded Sabina in agitation.

Each one looked at the other. Then a deadly silence came between them.

Hymn of the Sands

Within days, she was leaving Alexandria.

Sabina tossed her clothes into the suitcase and looked at the paintings that hung on the walls of her room as though they were clinging there for fear of being taken away. She grabbed a painting of the Lighthouse of Alexandria that left her with a feeling of desire, an upwelling that came in waves and a fevered heat burning inside her that made her tremble. It wasn't only her father that was making her leave: an insistent desire drove her to flee, to leave everything, to put her love for Luka to the test, as though she were impelled toward the unknown by a hidden force. So it's back to Italy then, to return to the house she left behind, the one overlooking the green mountains. The rest she'll leave in God's hands.

She went out to the entrance hall, and found her father sitting and staring off into space in silence, unaware of her presence and the sound of her footsteps. No, she won't ask him if she can stay in Alexandria, she won't be weak in front of him. She approached him and stretched out her hand with affection, patted his shoulders, and said in a voice filled with sorrow, "As you wish, father." Then she headed toward the door.

She went to the flower seller, who smiled and greeted her warmly, as usual. She concealed a tear that flowed over her cheek, and asked him for an orchid, the flower that Luka used to have delivered to her. She didn't want to tell him that she was leaving for good. She crossed the Corniche, and then hurried quickly to the beach. She leaned humbly over the sands of Camp Caesar Beach. She laid the orchid down gently and gazed at its colors, becoming engrossed in the beauty of its shape. She whispered to it with heart-felt emotion:

> May you always remember me, sands!
> And may you yearn for me, ocean waves!
> And weep at my departure, O winds and clouds!
> And may you remain in love with me forever, Luka!

She got up and began to run and run, as though the waves wanted to overtake her, and when they receded, they snatched her flower in their embrace and took it far out to sea. She set out on her way again. She circled around Raml Station, and roamed the city streets, looking at the taverns, and listening to snatches of an old Italian song:

> *Don't forget your pink coat*
> *But leave your hat behind,*
> *So I can keep the scent of your hair*
> *When you've left me for another. . . .*

In a daze as though she were lost, she found herself returning to Raml Station. She entered the Cecil Hotel and ordered a coffee. She noticed a phone booth in the hotel lobby:

should she call Luka? Should she tell him that she will be leaving the country and leaving him behind? She went outside. The sea breeze brushed over her. It lifted the hem of her dress, which she straightened out with her fingers. She thought about getting into a taxi but hailed a horse-carriage instead, as though she were a defeated princess passing among her people. She climbed up and sat down, stretching out her full length and resting one leg over the other. With a voice filled with the joy of defeat, she ordered the coachman to head in the direction of Safiya Zaghloul Street. The carriage bumped along the middle of al-Habib Street, then swung around to pass in front of her old school with its high walls and lofty trees that leaned affectionately against its walls, the Catholic church, houses of friends, the mansions she used to dance in, and the embassies she was invited to.

A shudder passed through her limbs when she remembered that her father would be alone: after he lost her mother, who had died in an accidental landmine explosion in al-Alamein, she was all he had left. Oh, Sabina, weren't the cruelty of those days enough for him?

Sawsan

I was too late to get to school on time, but I decided not to return home right away. I didn't like my studies, and I was lured away by the desire to discover the world around me. I noticed Budur at the bus station. She told me she was on her way to the workshop, and I asked if I could come with her. She hesitated and asked me, "But what about school?"

I gave her a scornful look. "Forget about it. The bell already rang so the doors are locked."

21

Girgis was busy when we entered, so Luka welcomed us with a smile, "Please come in. Mrs. Girgis, isn't it?"

I saw that Luka was interested in her from the first instant, so I thought Girgis would ask her to leave but he didn't. On the contrary, he was happy, and in the end we all went out together—Budur, Girgis, Luka, and I—and had lunch at Café Riche. It was a beautiful day, but it ended with a fight between me and my mother. She scolded me and was on the verge of hitting me. She would have, if I hadn't sworn to her on Said's life, and threatened her, saying, "When he gets back, I'm going to tell him how badly you treated me!" She cried and left me alone.

The neighbors say that Budur disappeared four days ago, and no one knows where she has gone. On my way home from school, I met Girgis at the corner of the alley. I asked him how he was and about Budur, and he confirmed the rumors for me. I didn't tell him about the conversation between Budur and Luka during the short time he stepped away from us in the Café Riche. That's when Luka asked her to go with him to Alexandria. She smiled, saying that she would think about it. Luka ended the conversation by putting his hand on hers, and she let him. When Girgis returned, I saw her quickly pull her hand away. I'm sure Girgis saw what I saw, but he pretended he hadn't.

Another day, I saw Budur getting out of a taxi, wearing a new dress. Her coloring had changed a lot from the sun and sea air.

The word "Alexandria" stirs up something in me; I imagine the wide seas and remember the time my father traveled there when I was a child: he brought me back a small white ball that bounced when it struck the ground, as well as a bright-colored headscarf. He told me it was from Zanqat al-Sittat outdoor market. I laughed. His body was sunburned. He told me to peel the dead skin from his shoulders, and I felt happy as I removed it and felt the moist layer of new skin underneath it.

She gestured to me, "Come here. I want you. I brought you something nice."

My mother wasn't at home so I went out to her, and found that she was crying. On her face and hands there were scratches. I asked her what happened, and she answered with a sob, "Girgis hit me because I traveled to Alexandria with the khawaga, although he knew I was there for work."

"Girgis knew you were in Alexandria?"

"Yes, I don't do anything without his permission."

"But why did you go to Alexandria with the khawaga?"

"Because he wants to open a women's clothing store there."

So what made Girgis upset? Why did he allow her to go if he didn't want. . . . If he didn't want the people in the neighborhood to make fun of him, saying, "You can't keep her happy or something?"

"What do people want from us?" Budur burst out. "Everyone should mind their own business, and like they say, "Let the guilty one take the hint!"

I knew how she must feel. I also knew that she loved Girgis, and that he loved her, and that there was a mutual trust between them. But Luka the khawaga had come between them and muddied the clear water of their lives.

I tried to lift her spirits by asking about the gift she had brought me from Alexandria. She presented me with a scarf and a nightgown, and said, "Wear the scarf when you go outside. And the nightgown—keep it for your trousseau when you get married." I blushed in embarrassment.

The neighbors suspected that my mother had lost her senses out of grief over Said: she had begun to talk to herself, and sometimes she would put her head out of the window of the apartment and call out at the top of her lungs, "Come here, Said! Haven't you been out long enough? Look how late it's gotten! I don't know where you are or what you're up to. Come here, Muhammad! Son, your mother has been worried about you for a long time now. For my sake, Said, come here, dear! You'll die of cold." And she would imagine that he was shouting back, "What do you want? I'll be up in a little bit, mother! Just five minutes: I'm talking to Muhammad about something."

One time we were walking on the street, on our way back from the market, when suddenly she turned to one of the soldiers passing by, and called to him, "Hey there, son."

"Yes, ma'am."

"You're in the army, right?"

"Yes, ma'am."

"You don't happen to know a young man who looks like you, by the name of Said Abd al-Qader? He entered the military six years ago and didn't come back. And now here we are, the war is over, and he hasn't returned."

"Ma'am, the war isn't over, so long as the Israelis are occupying our land."

"But you haven't seen Said, have you, young man?"

"No, ma'am, I'm based in Dahshur, not in the Suez. But in any case, give me his name and rank. I'll ask about him and let you know, insha'allah."

The soldier was being kind, and he was patient with my mother, but I felt that he was directing his words at me. He told us that he had recently graduated with a business degree and now was doing his military service. I knew he lived in Victoria Square, where I used to go when I was a child. I would lie on its green grass and look at the sky and clouds. I would think about the Creator of the Universe and imagine him on his throne. I would whisper to him and ask him to bring my brother back to me, and to cure my mother of her hallucinations. Would I be close to him if I rode a plane and flew up high? Does he love me? If I die, will I see him? I only came back to reality when I heard the gardener ordering me to get off the grass.

Budur

Budur sat by the window, leaning one of her arms on the sofa cushion. The sun had set, and an unaccustomed peace and quiet had settled over the alley: no children were playing outside, and there were no street vendors making their rounds. Even the stores hadn't reopened their doors after the afternoon siesta. She wanted to see people's faces, even if they had a look of contempt or disapproval. Her neighbors on the street judged by appearances. Why should it bother them if a woman works outside the house?

Sometimes she dreams of moving and living in another city like Alexandria. It's a beautiful city, with air that restores to the soul the happiness stolen from it. Just looking out on the sea is enough to transport a person to another world, one purer and more peaceful. She read in the Old Testament that in the beginning the Lord had his throne upon the water.

Luka gave her an opportunity to see the sea, so was she wrong when she accepted his invitation? She chided herself, *Why did he insist on taking me with him to Alexandria?* Then she whispered vainly to herself—I'm beautiful, and haven't I benefited from this beauty of mine? I want to live a better life. Girgis is a good man, and he trusts me. But he is a man, and he guards his honor jealously, especially when people talk about him.

—Luka told me when we were in Alexandria: "We can help each other. Things will change: you will be rich." At the same time, he told me I looked like Cleopatra! He told me she had eyes like mine, and that she loved two men who both worshiped her. They surrendered before the powerful throne of her beauty and her charms: "She was a clever woman, just like you!"

—What he did mean by that, that she loved two men? Is he trying to tell me something? I love Girgis, and I don't deny that I like Luka's personality. There is a great sorrow inside him, and his sad brown eyes are like those of my father who died when I was young. There is a tenderness in them that sends me to magical unknown worlds—like the world of the lake I saw when I was a young girl. They wear down my resistance and draw me close to them. I tried asking him what he meant. He gave me a hesitant look that wavered between the ocean's waves and my eyes that were fixed on him, and told me, "Cleopatra loved Egypt, and I love Egypt too." But what does Egypt have to do with anything? I want to know: does he love me or not?

"I want to own a clothes store," she had told him. "I have a lot of ideas, but this thing is tying me in knots. I feel like I'm locked in the cage of the past while worrying about the future." He had smiled and said, "Don't worry. I'll put an end to your anxiety. Forget about the past." Then he kissed her forehead.

When she played with the sand with her fingers, she felt a chill flow through her body, mixed with the warmth coming from Luka's fingertips as he clung to her hand. She couldn't keep herself from surrendering. She wished she had seen it coming. She remembered Girgis and shivered. Luka noticed it and felt alarmed, saying, "So do you want a confession? Yes, I want you beside me. I need someone to stand beside me. I don't want anything from you; I only want you by my side. I won't be a heavy burden on you: I'm over fifty, and I've gone through a lot of difficult times—don't believe that I haven't been hurt on the inside."

—He told me his story, and I was torn. I felt I was getting entangled with him. But should I tell Girgis? Impossible. He wouldn't understand. He wouldn't understand the essence of this relationship: he would think that there is something more than just sincere feelings.

Sawsan

I, too, was no longer considered a little girl: I had turned sixteen. I look in the mirror at my body that has now filled out: I know how much of an effect it has on others. The girls in school always tell me, "You have nice legs, Sawsan. Men will be fighting over you." I always like to go walking with my friends after school. We go to the Shubra Roundabout neighborhood where there is the al-Amir Fish Restaurant and kushari shops packed with students. When we leave the

27

restaurant, we notice the girls from the Good Shepherd School: I used to be so jealous of them, and hoped I could make friends with one of them. Most of them have big cars and drivers waiting for them. I used to imagine I was a daughter from a rich family. I would joke with my schoolfriends and tell them, "My father has a car like that one parked in front of the Good Shepherd." "Quit bragging!" my friend would answer, and we would laugh. We would start walking in front of al-Sahafa Coffeeshop to get some admiring glances from the young men sitting there, as well as the kisses we would snatch from them along with the smoke from their water-pipes. We would see pensioners in front of the post office and the Yacoub Abadir shoe stores, and we would eat rice pudding from Bunduq Dairies. We would watch newcomers to Cairo, fresh off their buses as they exited the station called "Menufiya Airport." We would amuse ourselves with the rotary dial on the phone beside the telephone exchange building, as we called up strangers we might know at some point in the future. We would smell the odor of grilling meat wafting from the Abu Azam Restaurant that made us feel hungry and poor. We would stare at the golden trinkets of Max the khawaga, until he chased us away with a wave of his fingers covered with diamond rings. It was a trip I made every day by myself or with my friends.

My Father

My father always took pride in Abd al-Nasser. He would say, "He's the one who gave us dignity among the nations. If it weren't for him, we would be like a chicken leg between the jaws of the Americans and English." Then he would sing

28

a tune of Abd al-Halim Hafez: "You pass over the desert and it becomes green . . . ." I was amazed by the president's magical power, as though he were a jinn who could turn a dry wasteland green.

My mother told me that the day Abd al-Nasser offered his resignation, my father was holding a drinking jug. He threw it high up in the air, and its broken parts scattered everywhere, cutting her eyebrow. He was no longer able to control himself, and that's when she tried to joke with him, declaring that politics is of no use, and that it was a waste of his time to listen to news reports. And what did he do but hit her and leave the house! Whenever I saw her scar, I remembered my father and Abd al-Nasser.

My father was always neatly dressed, clean-shaven, and with lustrous hair. Despite the fact that he used to come back late from the factory, he would insist on reading to me two suras from the Qur'an—"The Event" and "Ya-Sin"—telling me there were great blessings in both. He never hurt anyone in his life, in word or in deed. He always used to joke with the neighbors, but he never invited anyone to our house, since he was jealously protective of my mother. When sleep overcame him, he fell into a deep slumber, and if he woke up late, he insisted on going to the factory, only to return an hour later, saying, "The guard locked the factory door in my face." Then he would sigh, "Never mind. I've been docked a day's pay." He would stretch out beside my mother, who would get up quickly and say, "I'll go to the market."

He liked staying up late at home, and when he was happy, he sang for us. My mother would scold him, saying, "People are sleeping!" But he didn't care; he just replied, "Soon enough we'll all be taking the long sleep."

He died. Whenever I sit down to eat—my mother and myself—I would remember how he would pass up food and give me his share. He would say, "Sawsan is studying, and she needs energy. As for this boy Said, the Lord will provide for him." My father left, and Said left. Nothing was left to us but memories that filled the corners of the house and a picture on the wall: it was him on the beach surrounded by a group of friends filled with youth and vitality. Through his self-confident pose, he gave me a smile filled with happiness and contentment. How often I regretted that I wasn't in his arms in that photograph.

Queen Victoria

Sawsan didn't know why the square in the middle of the district where she lived, which she frequently crossed and sat in on her own or with Budur, was called "Victoria." When she asked, she was told that a beautiful Christian lady named Victoria used to live in a big house located on this square. She had inherited the substantial property from her husband, but the disobedience of her sons drove her to madness. She used to go out on her balcony after the Friday prayer and throw fruit and household objects at the passersby below, shouting, "I took care of you! I am a saint! I am Princess Victoria! I will forgive your sins, mankind!" Budur said, "When my mother saw this woman she was frightened, and believed that my grandmother had returned. She told me not to go there and she washed our house with Nile river water mixed with myrrh and soapworts flower. Then she got out a tray and on it she put bread, fuul beans, salt, and yogurt, and in the middle of it she placed a candle. She lit incense and left a knife and a Bible under my pillow to drive away my grandmother's spirit so it wouldn't make me mad." Despite that, Budur and Sawsan used to sneak off and go to the square, but they were never lucky enough to catch sight of the mad woman. Some said that she grew feeble in her old age and came to depend on her servant, a nun from one of the convents. Others claimed that her sons put her away in an asylum. But in the opinion of most people, she died and was buried beneath the square where she ordered a shop for the flower-seller to be built. The flower shop really was built, and then later, the Nasr al-Islam Mosque.

Once Sawsan asked a neighbor who was teaching her arithmetic, and who couldn't stop making advances on her during the lesson. He said, "When Queen Victoria decided to visit Egypt, she promised that she would visit the Shubra district, because it had the greatest number of Christians, and inasmuch as she was a protector of the Church, it was an honor for the Egyptians and the Christians of Shubra that the Queen was visiting them. The people of the district made preparations; they beautified the square with a flower garden and gave it the Queen's name. But unfortunately, she didn't come, or perhaps she visited Egypt but didn't come to Shubra—not to Saint Theresa nor any other church. But the square kept her name." From time to time, Budur used to think back on the old lady Victoria and say, "She was a lot like my grandmother." Then tears would well up and she would say to Sawsan, "Maybe I will meet the same fate."

"You're already completely crazy," Sawsan responded. And they would laugh.

Sawsan

Sawsan usually wore a dress without stockings. Despite the cold of winter, she would feel happy when she saw her shapely white legs. Her aunt Emmeline, who had bronze-colored skin and short dark black hair, loved her very much and would give her some of the sandwiches she had made for her twin sons, Sharif and Ihab. Sawsan remembered her chic black dress and her shiny new shoes, which she noticed when she leaned over to pick up a pen she had dropped.

Emmeline would defend her when the gym teacher hit her for being late. "Sawsan is bright and a good student," she would tell him, "but she lives far from school. I beg you, please go easy on her." The gym teacher—who punished her for her repeated lateness by hitting her—hadn't realized the efforts she made to get to school. Sawsan was struck with fear whenever she woke up late: she would look for her things and her wrinkled dress which she had forgotten to send to the ironer (actually, because she didn't have the money to pay for the ironing). Then she would run as fast as she could from Workshop Street to Canal Street, past the pharmaceuticals factory, where she would smell the odor of medicines that enveloped the overcast winter sky. Then Abd al-Hamid al-Deeb Street, where she saw workers sipping tea in cafés, a newspaper vendor calling out, the greengrocer stacking his produce, the horse that leans beside the factory (and the pungent smell of its urine), the pottery workshop, and she would run and run until she reached the massive tree beside the school. She used to vie with its sparrows every morning, begging the doorkeeper to let her in, as she saw the students going upstairs to the classrooms to the beat of a drum and to the words of the song, "Draw the blade! Awake! Awake!" She never took its meaning seriously, but for a reason she couldn't explain, it sent a shiver of enthusiasm through her body whenever she heard it.

Her school days passed by, and the gym teacher never hit her again. Sawsan got her secondary school diploma and applied to the French Department at Cairo University's College of Humanities. She was nervous and flustered the day she turned in her application and asked Budur to go with her.

Finally, the university! A new life—and a greater hurdle for her to cross. No school uniform after today: she could wear whatever clothes she liked. But when she entered the university, she was stunned. Her clothes seemed like faded old rags compared to the outfits she saw. She certainly wasn't the only one who had that feeling creep up on them, but she only saw herself. When she told Budur how she felt, she said, "It's no concern of yours: you're sweet, girlfriend—as beautiful as the moon. It's up to you, brain or no brain. You forget that I'm the owner of a clothes shop now. God brought us the khawaga Luka, then he took me under his wing."

The Clothes Boutique

Although Budur had begun spending most of her time in Alexandria after taking responsibility for the women's clothing store there, she maintained her relationship with Sawsan. She used to relax with her from time to time and tell her about the things that happened to her there, the women she met, and their personal quirks. At first, Budur was ignorant about a number of things, especially the way to treat women from the upper classes, although she learned quickly how to win their trust. She lived a different life with Luka, a life outside the restricted world she grew up in, a world that was more stimulating, but also thornier. If she wasn't careful, she occasionally made a mistake; other times she got it right.

Girgis was happy with the new situation. His manner of living didn't bother him, except for the lack of children. Budur's infertility used to make her weak to the point of dizziness, and she would go to the church and tell the priest about what was going on inside her. He would advise her that she should take the path she thinks is best for her, that she should trust her heart, and that Christ is always within her, and that she should let Him be her guide. She tried all kinds of ways to distract Girgis from thinking about infertility, and to make him feel that she was a complete woman she mastered the art of creating desire in him and renewing it. And when he came back from work exhausted, he would find her waiting for him at the dinner table, her body fresh and delicate. She would sit at his feet and kiss his brow. Pleasure would flow through his limbs, and a feeling of elation would enter into them. He would take her in his arms. When body clings to body, there is only room there for love. As time passed, they both succeeded in avoiding the subject; each one pretended to forget their grief. They immersed themselves in love and work and making money. He felt stirrings of suspicion sometimes when Luka's name was mentioned, but except for that, they dreamed of getting rich, buying a house to live in and starting a clothes boutique. In the morning, he drinks tea and goes to work.

A Wailing Wall

Luka's circumstances changed after the October War. He hadn't sided with Israel against Egypt, but he felt something break apart inside him, and he couldn't understand what it meant. The days of the '67 War hadn't gone too badly for him, in spite of his feelings of loneliness and fear. One night, as he was returning from work, he imagined that someone was following him. The air was cold and most of the shops had closed up early. He quickened his pace, looking for a way to escape. He entered the Estoril restaurant and left by the back door that opened onto the Qasr al-Nil passageway. He found himself on Talaat Harb Street, and continued in the direction of Talaat Harb Square. Now he was certain he wasn't imagining it, and that the man was trailing him like his shadow. He lit a cigarette; the smoke trailed upward and hung motionless in space. He felt his heart pounding faster. He wanted to disappear from sight, to hide somewhere—even in a garbage bin—but failed to find a place. Then suddenly he remembered Emmanuelle, a Greek friend of his mother who lived on Talaat Harb Square in the Groppi Building. He headed in that direction and finally reached the building; he climbed the stairs without looking behind him and knocked on the door. After a few moments that felt like an eternity, a gray-haired old woman opened the door. Traces of past beauty remained on her face, despite her filled-out features. Without hesitation, he slipped through the crack in the door, sweat pouring off him and fear coursing through his limbs.

"Luka, how nice to see you. . . . What's wrong? Is someone after you? What's happened?

"No—nothing."

"Relax, I'll get you a glass of water."

"No, no, I don't want any water. Just look out the window for me, but don't let anyone see you. Take a look: is there a tall man wearing a black jacket standing in the square or on the street below?"

With slow, heavy steps, she walked to the window and cautiously pulled back the edge of the curtain; then she came back, wearing the same worried expression. Although she had seen someone standing in the square, she pretended she hadn't, so as not to tax Luka's nerves any more than they already were.

"There's no one there," she said calmly. "Don't worry about it: maybe it was a pickpocket, or an admirer following you."

"No, it's not a pickpocket. I know I'm being watched—but *you* know I have no contact with Israel nowadays. They tried to recruit me, but I refused. Maybe at first I felt some sympathy for Israel, and I had some delusions about the idea of establishing a state for Jews, but now I mind my own business. I have nothing to do with anything. I want to stay in Egypt, I don't want to travel to Israel, and I don't want to be a spy."

"The Egyptian secret police aren't stupid, Luka, so be careful."

Emmanuelle was also Jewish, and while she was still alive, his mother had frequently asked her to take care of him. She would ask about him and knew all about what he was doing, but as she grew on in years and Luka's visits to her became less frequent, she began to forget about him. Although her sons had emigrated to Israel, she preferred to remain in Egypt: she knew the country well, and had spent the most beautiful years of her life there. Now she lived a quiet life in downtown Cairo. What would she find in Israel? The life she had left in her wouldn't allow her to start over again. She led a settled life in Egypt: she woke up in the morning, went out to the street, bought the papers and some magazines, drank her morning coffee at Groppi's or at the Continental in Opera Square; she met some of her friends, and then went back home at lunchtime. Before the 1967 War, when the Mossad had tried to recruit Luka, he went to her, trembling in fear, to ask her for advice. They spoke a lot about the nation, about Egypt, Greece, and Israel, about their shared sorrows and divided sympathies. About how they had suffered because the government was afraid of them, and because it treated them as a source of anxiety, even though their nationalist sympathies had been shaken in the face of the dream of Greater Zionism. They came to the conclusion that night that they had no nation other than Egypt: they loved its Nile, they felt affection for its people, and they spoke its language. As for Israel, let it be what it is. Emmanuelle had saved him that night, and on other nights when panic seized him. With him, she lived through his aborted love story, and her being there was one reason why he didn't go to pieces after Sabina's escape to Italy.

After he had calmed down a little, he asked her, "Do you think the Egyptian secret police know about the Mossad's attempt to recruit me?"

"I don't think so: the government's been preoccupied with the corruption that led to the defeat. Forget the whole thing for now. I'll make some dinner for you and then you can go to sleep. You shouldn't go back out on the street at such a late hour." Then she gave him a small prayerbook with pages from the Old Testament and told him, "Read these words before you sleep, and you'll fall asleep restfully and quietly. It will put your fears to rest."

Luka lay down and read, "The Lord is my rock, my fortress, and my salvation . . . . In Him I find my refuge, my rescue, and my deliverance from evil. . . . For waves of death have surrounded me . . . floods of perdition have frightened me, the heights of the chasm encompassed me. . . . In my anguish I have called out to the Lord, and cried out to my God, and from His temple, he has heard my voice. . . . The earth trembled and shook because of his wrath."

Luka didn't sleep that night, and the jinn danced on the edge of the blanket while in his head he imagined them hanging from the window curtains. Memories leaped into his imagination like a movie reel projected onto the ceiling of the white room: Sabina, who had left forever, without giving him the opportunity even to say goodbye, he had only seen her from afar walking up the ship's gangplank: she was wearing a diaphanous blue dress with a white hat. Sabina seemed fragile and defeated. Despite the harbor crowds, he was able to get close to the ship just at the moment it pulled away from Alexandria, the moment the past separated from the present, the moment history ended. Alexandria, which she was passionate about, and which she loved to draw in her nature sketches. He remembered how she used to take him with her on trips to the ruins on the city's outskirts, how she used to dream of rebuilding the Library of Alexandria and its lighthouse. She would laugh, saying, "I want to immortalize Alexandria in my paintings—and you can immortalize me with your love." Oh, Sabina! Why did you leave?

Her father had told him, "If you marry her, you will marry her as a Christian; I don't want to marry off my daughter to a Christ-killer." "But I didn't kill Christ—I never laid eyes on him," Luka thought. "I'm not the traitor Judas. Why am I burdened with the guilt of my ancestors? I wasn't there when they condemned Christ. I didn't see them when they raised him on the cross, leaving him to hang there between heaven and earth."

Luka put his face between his hands, then floated in the extreme darkness as he imagined that the words of Sabina's father were true, and that they were dragging him to the gas-chamber, and that he was choking to death. Then, as they burned Sabina and her children before his eyes, the stench of burnt flesh filled his nostrils, and terrible visions followed one after another until he fell asleep.

Salim

At the university, Sawsan learned the meaning of freedom— opinions, ideas, demonstrations, student groups, and slogans: groups that called for shar'ia law, wearing the hijab, dividing the sexes, and placing the nation under religious authority; demonstrations against Israel and against the peace treaty; pamphlets agitating for war and vengeance for the lives of young Egyptian and Palestinian martyrs; and other statements declaring that Israel doesn't want peace, only a truce in order to recover from the blow of the Yom Kippur defeat. Some say that Sadat is a traitor while others declare that he is a shrewd man, capable of dealing with difficult challenges, since someone like him who was part of the leadership of the Revolution would never sell Egypt out, no matter what.

Amid this ideological back-and-forth she became friends with someone they called "Marx," although his real name was Salim. He was a student of English literature, and she always saw him in the cafeteria. He was the only one who was interested in listening to her. His opinions were unusual but logical: he would talk about equality among the classes, about workers and capital, about the proletariat and the working classes. He hated the United States, and loved Baudelaire: he asked her to read *Fleurs du Mal*. "Where are we now?" he would say. "We are marginalized and poor. No sooner do we emerge from a catastrophe than we head into a labyrinth."

Salim had grown up in a religious family: his father was an al-Azhar scholar who insisted on giving him a proper religious upbringing, and he always used to tell him, "You must do your utmost so that God may stand by your side and come to your aid. Truly, He gives to both the wicked and the pious, but in the end He will distinguish between the two."

Salim performed his ritual ablutions and muttered the words that would perhaps drive away the spirit of Satan within him, he carried his books, went to the university, sat in the study hall, and listened to the professors saying, "Look at the telephone, radio, television: all these miracles of science have shortened time and distance. Darwin proved the idea that the world was created in six days is wrong. The earth required millions of years for life on it to develop. And missions to space haven't found God's heavenly throne, have they?"

"This is what is incompatible with the text of the Holy Qur'an," the philosophy professor went on to say, "that '*He created the heavens and the earth in six days and then sat upon the Throne.'"* Salim lifted his face up to heaven, abstained from eating, and wept in a dark room, asking himself:

—What does this professor know about the glory of God the Creator? Where is the truth? Is egalitarianism the answer? Living by the principle of reconciling the metaphysical and the material worlds, you have nothing to lose. If you can't be an angel, then at least be a human being in the service of humanity. Or so it seemed to Salim, as he read up on Sufism, Islamic jurisprudence, politics, and poetry.

In moments of anxiety and worry, Sawsan asked herself:

—Why exactly was I born in this alley, and why to these two parents? I want to be someone else, not Sawsan from Shubra, as they call me in the university—another Sawsan, from Zamalek or Heliopolis. I want to be anyone else but me. Studying alone won't be enough: it's up to me to improve my French and English in order to work in a foreign company or one of the luxury hotels. People won't respect me unless I'm wealthy. Never mind what Salim says, I have to do all I can to be like that.

Sawsan started going to the library to read what the authors that Salim talked about had written. When he told her that there can be no literature without philosophy, she read philosophy and got to know her way around the dictionaries and encyclopedias. She began to look at the world around her with new eyes. The library seemed like a familiar world, full of ideas and opinions. She loved its high walls and its lofty ceiling, and she would sit there for hours without getting bored, copying down information she found interesting. She would eat the lunch she brought with her and spend the rest of the day without eating. When she returned home, exhausted and pale, her mother would scold her, saying, "You'll die young."

I feel my freedom with Salim. I wasn't afraid of him, and I didn't hide from him the truth about me: where I live, or my social background. With the others, I used to be reserved and play a different role according to my social class. Despite the rumors floating around Salim—that he is a Marxist and an unbeliever—I haven't lost my esteem and respect for him. With him, I have come to realize that poverty isn't something bad, and perhaps it's an incentive for creativity. We've talked about everything: sex, sin, war, peace. He would say, "The body that contains you isn't important, what's important is the role you play."

As time passed, and my mind opened up, my view of Budur changed. I gladly accepted her gifts of clothes and other things after I became free of my self-consciousness, just as I accepted the situation she had chosen for herself: I no longer looked at her from the same narrow perspective. She was always traveling: the Free Trade Zone in Port Said, Alexandria, Suez. I used to see Girgis from time to time in the clothes boutique that they had recently succeeded in opening. He worked there diligently day and night: I would find out what she was doing, and ask him to say hello for me. Sometimes I would ask him to alter my clothes to match my size now that I had slimmed down.

Luka and Budur

Things were going very well for Luka. His relationship with Budur grew strong. He thought she had a good heart, and she filled the void created by the loneliness and anxiety he suffered from. Likewise, Budur bonded with him, not only because he supported her with the money she needed, but also because he could shake up the stagnation that enveloped her life; he killed the fear of the future that was inside her. Their relationship wasn't used to kisses and embraces. In the beginning, it was possible to yield to him but there was something inside her that prevented her from continuing. She would drop in on him in his apartment in the Camp Caesar district to wake him up. She would close the window that looked out over the blue sea and foam on the waves vying with the wind. She would see him sleeping, bare-chested, lying with his face near the window. His shoulder muscles were solid, and his body showed no evidence that he was in his fifth decade; he had vitality and beauty. She wanted to embrace him and sleep in his arms—maybe for an hour, or maybe the whole day. "My God, is there no redemption from sin? Confession is not a deliverance from evil. I know that he truly loves me, but so does Girgis!"

She was afraid to ask him why he was drawing her so close to him, and why he insisted on giving her everything. Why exactly has he placed so much trust in her? She remembered the first time they met, the way he looked at her, the unspoken messages those glances sent her way, the touch of his hands. At first, naively, she succumbed to all his flirtations, happy that her employer was flirting with her; not realizing the consequences, she encouraged him to continue. When he dared to plant a kiss on her neck, she trembled with an excess of emotion and ran off, leaving work that day, determined never to return to him. She didn't tell Girgis all the details, but made it clear that she wasn't comfortable with Luka.

Girgis didn't understand, and told her, "That's just the way he treats women—it doesn't mean anything. And anyway, he's an older man so you have nothing to worry about." How had things gotten to this point, that she had come to yearn to see him every morning? How had a spirit not her own come to dwell inside her, a spirit that loved him, loved his pain when he talked about Sabina, loved his fear of the unknown, loved his exaggerated defense of his Egyptianness, even though he knew no other homeland except Egypt, loved his jokes and witty remarks, and loved the way his hair falls on his forehead when he got upset. The image of her grandmother running to the lake and talking to the air and its phantoms appeared before her eyes. The only release, then, is submission or madness.

Adil and Fayza

I sit in my lonely room. I don't know what I can do to kill the boredom and desire within me. I look in the mirror and see a face not my own. I see my soul imprinted on the reflection of my image—my image that is also not my own. The black holes on the sides of the mirror remind me of the sadness that fills me. The walls are faded, the carpet is frayed, and my worn-out shoes rest beside the entrance to the room. I wonder: when will Said return? When will I enjoy intimacy with Salim?

I look out over our alley, and find our neighbor Adil reeling as he comes this way. A little later, I hear him quarreling with his father—the porter who transports goods on a three-wheeled cart and goes around barefoot, bent-backed, and wearing white sirwal trousers. His face has a look of determination and vitality, as though he were one of the pyramid builders. As usual, the quarrel ends with him kicking out his son and his friends, accompanied by his insults and curses. The young men head off, laughing and mocking the old man. A group of poor young men was filling up the alley with their ruckus: they have no qualms about harassing young women, assaulting passersby, extorting shop-owners, or getting into vicious fights with their peers from neighboring districts. Adil isn't that bad, as far as I'm concerned; he would be on his best behavior with me, and would get flustered when his eyes met mine. From time to time, he asks about me. He sits shyly on the edge of the sofa, assuring my mother that, "God willing, Said will come back safe and sound, auntie. Only Miss Sawsan should hurry up and get her degree." He has a hard time getting out what he wants to say, and sometimes he ends his visit with some incomprehensible words before heading out, while casting a fleeting glance my way.

"Who is this Adil?" Budur shrieked. "I'm getting sick of hearing about him! He's a lowlife, honey!" In vain, I tried to defend him to her, or even to myself. I would think about Adil with Salim's logic, and try to find excuses to dissuade him. I used to see him sitting for hours through the window of his room, looking serious as he stares out at nothing, as though he weren't part of this world, and so didn't hear the slanders of Hamdiya's mother and her terrible gossip about the girls of the alley—about one who lost her virginity, and another who was arrested with her lover, and a third who eloped with the mechanic—even though not much time had passed since the scandal involving her own daughter Hamdiya, who had eloped with her fiancé.

Sometimes I used to imagine that the police had arrested Adil, and as he is being shuttled back and forth between police stations, he pleads for a cigarette from one of his traveling companions, or wraps himself in an old blanket that he shares with one of them, or rests on his haunches beside a door of a train in Upper Egypt, his limbs frozen, but the only thing that worries him is his sister Fayza: he is afraid of her falling into vice. Poverty is a devil that seduces every woman who goes hungry. Fayza was the one who would always defend him in front of the police. Once I saw her take him in her arms while she shouted in their faces, "Shame on you! Leave this poor man alone—he hasn't left his room the whole night long!" The police officer shoved her away, and as her feet slipped, she fell to the ground while the car sped off with a shudder, trailed by Fayza's curses and pleas.

In conversation, Salim stresses that "Man is the center of the universe," and that "Action is supreme in human life. There is no contradiction between being religious and being civilized: if religious people renounce worldly life, then why do they go on living?" His talk—when I first met him— conflicted with the prevailing discourse at the university, where the campus was littered with pamphlets claiming that the laws by which nations are ruled are un-Islamic, and that "the separate peace with the Jews (the enemies of God) with all the rifts and divisiveness among the Arabs that result from it, is not a legitimate peace," and that "insulting Muslim religious scholars, belittling their status, and imprisoning them is an insult to Islam and Muslims," and that "the repeated claim that there is no religion in politics and no politics in religion is worthless," and that "associating oneself with trends that conceal a secret hostility to Islam is a suspect association." And there were other slogans, too, that were hostile to the social order. Salim would reiterate that although he objected to the thinking espoused by the student groups, he welcomed any solution that would bring about a measure of comfort to the nation's oppressed youth. When I asked him directly whether he belonged to the groups, he said, "I will support them if they provide us with change."

"I believe that utopias can never be achieved," I said, "Better that humanity should be satisfied with what they have been given. The ideal society is a fantasy. If the path to it is strewn with violence and bloodshed, I would refuse it."

"They have a plan," he said, "and they are on their way to achieving it."

"If it means a lot of bloodshed, then I reject it!"

I had begun to have doubts about everything. I felt fear, and a shudder ran through my body. I imagined him with a beard, carried on people's shoulders as he shouts out slogans crying for blood and clutches a sword that gleams in the dusty June sunlight. I imagined that when the treacherous bullets hit his bare chest, the faces of the shouting crowds turn into black circles swollen with blood-red veins. One time I felt overwhelmed and weak, and for the first time I felt afraid that he was by my side. I wanted to turn away, but he insisted on coming with me. We took the bus, and sat next to each other in silence. I absented myself by looking out the window that looked out over the streets and city squares. Our bodies were touching and warily, I didn't resist.

"I'll see you tonight at seven," he said. "We'll go to see some friends." I tried asking about them. "You'll find out when you get there," he said.

Salim

You stare hard at the mirror, running your hand over the stubble that has sprouted on your chin during the past few hours. You are ready to meet Sawsan. You put the brush in the soap dish and look at the soap bubbles gushing out of it, growing and swelling to the size of the sadness inside you. You will meet her today and you'll both go see a group of friends—perhaps you will make plans for a distant future that will change the life of the nation.

Salim eagerly placed the razor blade against his chin. His hands trembled and he cut himself. He splashed on a little water and it mingled with the blood. He smelled the blended scent of soap and blood. In primitive societies, a blood sacrifice was the only way to free the tribe from the wrath of nature and the curse of the gods. He took off his shirt, as his hungry cat walked between his legs. He could feel her warmth when her tail touched his legs. He imagined it was Sawsan, a cat craving love and fulfillment. To himself he whispered, "I'm not being fair to Sawsan. She doesn't have the background to get lost in the labyrinth of politics."

He examined his body in the mirror. Maybe he had put on a little weight, or maybe he'd lost a few kilograms, he couldn't say. He began to sigh out loud, but stopped abruptly, then puffed out his chest and flexed his muscles. He dropped his pants and stood on them. The cat hurried over to them and began to toy with them. He pulled them from her, and tossed them out of reach. He noticed traces of dried semen on them that he hadn't recalled being there. Was it the same woman with indistinct features, the one in whose long locks of hair he would get tripped up, her hair coiling and taking shape with every movement of desire: sometimes in African braids, sometimes flowing freely down her back? Was she light-skinned, or bronze-colored, or a fiery redhead? He couldn't say, but he felt sated and content.

Through the window of the room, the sun winked its eye at him, then dwindled and disappeared. He hated to see the sunset: it reminded him that everything comes to an agonizing end, where all colors revert to the invisible. Does he have the right to rebel? Is humanity naturally inclined to be unhappy? Why do people always consider the present the worst of times? Would a time come when circumstances would change or is it just a vicious circle? *Why did You create a thinking creature?* he wondered. He fastened his watchband around his wrist, and saw that it was time to go meet Sawsan. As he sauntered out, the cat was licking her private parts, her back legs in the air as she reclined back on his trousers. On the way he asked himself: —What do you want from Sawsan? And what does she want from you? We'll get married and become a conventional couple whose greatest concern is eking out a living and putting food on the table for the children. Then old age and senility, then a wooden casket in which we are carried through the neighborhoods we walked in when we were alive. What do I want?

Sawsan

Salim met me downtown by the Cosmopolitan Hotel. He was late enough that I was starting to get hungry and was planning to leave, but I hesitated. I thought I'd go to the Madbouli Bookstore or Dar al-Shorouk, but I changed my mind. I felt worried, and told myself he'd be angry. Salim arrived, but seemed flustered. "Come on," he said, "We're going to see my friends."

"Where are they?" I asked.

"At a comrade's house."

"I don't feel like visiting someone I don't know."

"Don't be a reactionary: they're intellectuals. We're just going to sit around and discuss general topics."

After some hesitation, I agreed. We took the bus; I felt nervous because it was so crowded, but I was happy to have his embrace and protection.

We crossed a wooden bridge; there were a few lights amid the darkness emitting their beams from a distance to light the road. I clung to Salim's warm hand and forgot my mother's warnings. We took a dusty country road that was empty of houses. I pressed hard on his fingers, and he told me, "Don't be afraid. We're almost there."

"Are there snakes in these fields?" I asked.

"No, there's no snakes," he responded quickly. "Just wolves."

I said nothing.

"Why are you looking at me like that?" he asked.

"You're an angel, not a wolf."

"Oh sure! But if we lay down on the ground now, would you still agree?"

I was taken aback by his suggestion, and couldn't think of anything to say in response, but I felt pleased that he desired me. "I was kidding," he said abruptly. "I know you're open-minded enough to take the joke. I'm just preoccupied." Because he was holding my hands, I couldn't resist, and I found myself pressing on them with all my love for him and all that kept me away from him. He removed his hands and wrapped me in his arms. I heard his heart beating, and breathed in the smell of him. I noticed nothing except the sound of a pack of stray dogs barking; they were panting after a bitch that was coquettishly strutting about. It was as if the pack were a divine intervention to break the tension. A young man who seemed surprised to find us there passed by us. To my astonishment, I found Salim warmly shaking his hand. I learned that he was Ihab al-Shinawi, his comrade in the university and in "the cell." He was very influential in the student union and was the one who recruited Salim.

We climbed the stairs, and a young man with a scowling face opened the door for us. Before we could get comfortable, he pointed at me, saying, "The sister will stay with the women in the room next door." I headed toward the parlor, which was empty except for a table and a wooden chair. There were no pictures on the walls, but tucked away in a corner there was a couch. I entered the room assigned to me, expecting to find all my friends, but contrary to what I thought, I only found three women who I couldn't get a good look at because they were wearing face veils.

They welcomed me with a few simple words and went back to their conversation, which had been interrupted by my entrance. They talked about a lot of things: the Iranian revolution, the Islamic caliphate, the rule of shari'a law, and the introduction of changes that would alter the position that Islam now found itself in. They talked about the example of Hasan al-Banna, who Muslims should take as a model for themselves, and whose life was cut short by assassination. They talked about takfir groups and other things. I felt out of place and the oxygen in the room seemed to rapidly dwindle away. I fidgeted in my seat, then I stood up, said goodbye to them, and turned to leave. I didn't wait for them to reply, but walked to where "the men" were sitting. They stopped talking, and Salim hurried toward me, saying, "Can you wait a little?"

"I've stayed too long. But don't worry, I'll get back on my own."

He looked pained. "You shouldn't go alone," he said. "We'll finish this thing very quickly. I'm sorry, everyone, but I have to go now." Ihab and he agreed to meet at the university, but I had already taken the stairs at lightning speed. The fields had grown darker: *Where am I? How did I get mixed up in these things? What are they planning?* I darted glances in every direction, and my mouth went dry. I recalled Budur and my mother. I walked aimlessly for a while, struggling to remember which way Salim and I had come. The frogs were making a sad monotonous croaking. The smell from the fields told me that the plants were releasing their nighttime moisture. The smell of mice filled my nose as they leapt into the water from the wooden bridge. The lamentations of crickets were deafening to my ears. I looked up to the sky and found the stars that had watched over me when I arrived. They were still in their lonely places, despite the clouds' attempts to conceal and smother them.

I heard his voice calling me. Despite my fear, his voice sent waves of calm through me and I stopped so he could catch up with me. He touched my trembling hand—it was cold.

"Who *are* you?" I burst out at him. "You're a liar and a schizophrenic! You preach one thing, but do another—you claim to be enlightened, but you're nothing but an extremist straying from the truth. I was wrong about you, just like everybody else. You go on about liberation and change while you're stuck with absolute certainty and inflexible ideas. You're bloodthirsty! You want to kill in order to create a utopia—a utopia that *you* won't make: others will and they'll impose their vision on you! Don't come near me! Get away from me, so I can see you for what you really are! Your speeches cast a spell on me and I gave in to your temptations. Who are those people? And how did they get to you? Are you going to stick with them to the end? Salim, you told me once that you would follow the devil if he was your guide to salvation. Is this the kind of salvation you want?"

"Don't be romantic. Revolution and bloodshed will renew the life of the people. In revenge there is life."

He continued making speeches, and little by little his voice grew distant until it dissolved amid the stars glimmering in the sky over the black fields.

Rusty Gates

"Cowards die many times before their deaths. The valiant never taste of death but once," he said, quoting Shakespeare as he sat sipping coffee in the al-Hurreya Coffeehouse on

Bab al-Luq Square. The shoeshine had just finished polishing his shoes.

He lit a new cigarette and stared into space, letting his ideas rise up along with the smoke. The suspicion that he would be arrested was taking shape before him in images—all of them horrible—and had reached the point that he was now convinced that his movements were being watched by people following him like his own shadow.

He was no longer that arrogant, naïve young man who would spout out talk about freedom, equality, fair distribution, and all the other slogans that used to stir up the student assemblies. After he had gotten to know Ihab, he had become withdrawn, giving terse responses to words directed at him, and no longer getting into discussions with people he didn't know.

He stopped thinking and asked himself: *Where is this path taking me?*

Voices rang out within the college building, as though the angel of death had descended to spread panic among mortals. Throngs of students were stirred up. In the trees whose verdant branches had so often given us shade, fires blazed. Soldiers broke through the students' ranks and cracked their clubs on our shoulders. Fevered shouts denouncing peace with the murderers of prophets grew louder, and smoke from the fires mingled with tear-gas. I was arrested, along with a large crowd who had the bad fortune to fall into the clutches of state security. Along with them, I found myself being led away, to who knows where.

In a room with rancid air, they sat me down on a wooden chair. From the glimmer of light coming through the solitary window, I could make out that I was not alone: Salim was there,

54

tied to the back of a chair with ropes that kept him tightly in place and prevented him from falling over.

"Why are you acting like revolutionaries?" the officer bellowed at us.

Then he turned to Salim, "You there, Mr. Big Shot! Who are you supposed to be—another Mustafa Kamil? Yeah, you, mama's boy!"

When he didn't respond, the officer nodded to one of his aides, who swiftly gave him a slap.

"Who are you with, you son of a bitch!"

"I'm not with anyone."

"Then how come you're in here?"

"I was expressing my opinion."

"Yeah, well, save your opinion for yourself, not for the university! Why are you stirring up public opinion against the government?"

"Because the country's policies conflict with the rights of the Palestinian people."

"What's that got to do with scum like you? It's none of your business. You people want to head right into war—one loss isn't enough for us. Look, son, tell me who you're with so you can go and sleep in your own home tonight."

"I told you, I'm not with anyone. I'm on my own."

"There's no need to keep it to yourself. Talking would be the best thing for you!"

He made no reply.

"So you don't want to talk!"

Salim still said nothing.

"Fine. I'll find out how to make you talk. Take him away."

Then the officer turned to me. He smiled, and then said, "How about that—a face like an angel but she does the devil's work." Then, taking a fatherly tone, he added, "I'm telling you, young lady, a rough place like this isn't for you. You really shouldn't be throwing away your future. Nice girls have no business in politics: he tricked you into it because you love him. It doesn't have to be like this. He's naïve, miss. You really have to make the right choice here. You're better off focusing on your studies, and forget about acting stubborn. You're already in enough trouble as it is."

I was ashamed of myself, and I couldn't look at him. Nerves and a powerful desire to weep overtook me. I was released on my own recognizance and allowed to return home after I signed a pledge not to participate in any activities opposed to the national interest. I had learned a lesson in "real" nationalism. Salim's detention was extended to forty-five days of investigative custody.

❖

Budur left the room and locked it behind her, leaving an amount of money on the table. Girgis got out of bed. His eyelids were so heavy he couldn't open them, and there was a light pain creeping up on his fingers. He gargled some water, then spat it out in the sink. He noticed the money, and wondered: *Why did she leave this cash here?* Then he picked it up and put it in the pocket of his robe. He changed his clothes and went off to work.

When she returned in the evening, he didn't ask her about the money or where she got it. He knew for sure it was Luka who gave it to her, but he didn't ask. For her part, she didn't ask him what he did with the money, the same as his father, after he left school and started working in stores and workshops. His father didn't care if he was still in school or not: the important thing was that he was bringing in cash, and when his mother cautioned his father, he replied, "Then what's the point of having sons? It's because they bring in money, so mind your own business!"

As a child, Girgis was thin and pale-skinned, and his mother used to make him do the fifty days of fasting, when they would eat no food that came from a living creature. The smell of oil would penetrate everything in the house. He used to hate fasting, and he would go eat kofta at a restaurant on al-Tur'a Street. His mother would smell it on him when he returned and tell him, "Christ will be angry with you." At night he would dream that Judas was putting him on the cross and hammering nails into his limbs and body.

Girgis didn't like his father and used to hate going to see him at the shop where he worked selling eggs on al-Warsha Street, since his classmates would make fun of him. "He's still a baby chick," they would say. "He hasn't hatched yet!" His anger at his father increased when he saw him flirting with a woman in the shop one day, and putting his hand on her breasts. His father spotted him, but showed no embarrassment about it, and kept right on doing it. "Wise up, smart guy, like your old man," his father told him, "and don't go telling your mother." Even after he grew up, he couldn't shake the image of his father whenever he touched a woman's breasts, but it gave him a special kind of enjoyment.

He wanted to erase the cross tattooed on his wrist A friend advised him to go to the blacksmith. The blacksmith put a drop of molten iron on his wrist, and then with a piece of dirty cloth he removed the cross, as skin and blood mingled in the cloth. He lost a lot of blood, which would have killed him, if it weren't for his mother who took him around to all the tombs of saints and holy men, "since *healing comes from God*," as they say. He felt liberated after removing the tattoo. He had become a human being like everyone else he met— no more, no less.

He himself informed Budur that he was in love with a Muslim girl and wanted to marry her. So he took another name, and they went to the maazun, who noticed the place where the cross had been on his hand and asked him about it. He got flustered and the whole affair became a public scandal. The girl threatened to kill herself, and none of her family's attempts to end her love for him succeeded, until they sent her to a fortuneteller, who informed them that she was possessed by a demonic spirit, and that only a priest familiar with these lowly matters could exorcise it. They summoned a priest who read certain passages from the Good Book that drove the evil spirit out through her toes. She recovered and no longer needed to see Girgis. When Budur heard this story, she laughed. She would remind him of it from time to time. "Our Lord blessed her," she said with a mocking smile, "and afflicted me!"

Girgis

What should I do?" Girgis asked himself. *"Should I lock the doors on her? Should I imprison her in a locked room? Should I hit her, beat her, cut her hair, and break her skull? Should I burn her body?*

—Then he muttered to himself, "I'm not capable of anything like that: I love her and I can't abuse her—she's passionate, reckless, and greedy for everything. She wants money, love, and power. If I want to control her, I shouldn't give her the opportunity to get free. Her wings will be strong and she'll fly away, soaring far off, and leave me for another man. I'll break her legs so she can't leave. . . . She doesn't listen to what I have to say at all now. She says, do you want to lock me up inside these four walls, and me with no children? Her words, her disobedience, are an insult to my manhood. Money has let her dominate me. She's grown powerful and I've become weak."

Girgis walked the whole length of Shubra Street, then passed through the tunnel: fear swept over him whenever a train passed above him. He walked down Ahmad Urabi Street and ate a sandwich at al-Tabie, then took Imad al-Din followed by Talaat Harb. He was drawn to the lights of Cinema Miami, but didn't cross the street. He walked along Adli Street, passing by al-Ahly Bank and then the synagogue. He wanted to go see Luka at work but he put off the idea. Crossing the street, he found himself in front of the Cap D'Or bar on Abd al-Khaliq Tharwat Street and went inside. He sat down and drank heavily. Then he stood up, and in a sobbing voice, asked, "What did I ever do to make him take my wife from me? I was loyal to him, I swear I didn't steal! I swear I never ripped him off. Is this what you get in return for loyalty?"

"It's not men you should blame," shouted back a voice from a corner of the room, "It's women, you idiot!"

"No—not my wife, she's not to blame. He's the one who seduced her. She's just a poor woman, I swear to God. . . .

It's just her thinking that gets her into trouble. She has a very noble soul. She wants to rise above it all."

Then the room started spinning, so that speaking became too much for him, and he flung himself down on the seat and propped his head against the wall, staring at nothing.

He really had been loyal to Luka. He did whatever Luka told him to do, he never once demanded a raise, and he didn't think about leading an independent life. He was satisfied. When he went down to the coffeeshop, he would brag about Luka to his friends, telling them that, "the man is the ultimate in sophistication." He used to like him, he liked his appearance and the way he smelled, so much so that he once asked him what kind of cologne he used. When he found out that it was expensive, he held off on buying it, but the same day, he was surprised when Luka placed the cologne on the table in front of him, and told him, "This is a gift from me to you."

The waiter tapped him on the shoulder, saying, "My friend, there are three things you can't rely on: money, even if you have a lot of it; a ruler, even if you're close to him; and a woman, even if you've known her a long time."

Then one of the drunks started laughing and shouted out, "Women might ditch a spineless man like you, but *my* wife sticks with me!"

An Empty Carriage

Although Said had been gone for years, his mother didn't lose hope that he would return from the front. Separation had made her more eager to see him, and longing for him made her more patient and hopeful that she would meet him again.

People in the alley believed she had lost her mind for good, whether or not Said ever returned. She used to wake up early in the morning and go to the train station, crowded with the faces of people coming and going, and she would describe to them what Said looked like. She sometimes found someone who listened to her and sympathized with her sad tale, but most times she was met by indifferent shrugs, as they all went on their way.

Once, one of them told her that there was a train at the station carrying soldiers, and that perhaps her son was among them. He led her to a darkened railway car, grabbed her hands, and jumped on her. She tried to escape and shouted, but he was quick to stifle her breath with his own warm breath. No one had kissed her since her husband had died. He was strong and ravenous, and he pressed up against her with all his weight, and she staggered underneath him, his miserable and wretched victim. Her body, which hadn't been touched since Sawsan's father died, creaked and resisted, but fear of God's wrath gave her an unusual strength to get him off her. Yet the man was insistent and pressed on her with greater force. With mechanical motions he tried to release himself of his desire, but she succeeded finally in driving him off, and she bolted away until she reached the door of the railway car. She began to run and let out a choked cry like a confused bird that had escaped from a hunter after a prolonged struggle. After this incident, Said's mother stopped going to the train station, and for a long while she didn't leave the house.

Veronica

Luka grew more interested in Budur, although his first love for Sabina had not diminished. When he felt sad, he recalled her, and she came to him, with her beautiful eyes. He remembered their hands entwined on Alexandria's Miami Beach, and her smile that would turn reality into a true heaven, like the happiness of Adam and Eve before the fall.

Ten years earlier, Luka had become friends with an Italian woman named Veronica, who had a close, almost familial relationship with Sabina's relatives. She worked for a business that sold works of art, rare pieces of furniture, and old books and manuscripts. She would visit Egypt from time to time to take part in auctions. She considered Egypt itself an open showroom, and would say that Egypt had made her rich, since the whole world's treasures could be found there. "History began here," she used to say, "and it will end here too."

Luka used to help her out by introducing her to some of the customers he dealt with. Although Luka sometimes doubted Veronica's intentions, he had nevertheless convinced himself to trust her. When she unexpectedly married an Italian businessman who lived in New York and moved there to live with him, his connection with her was almost severed—until a year before, when he suddenly saw her in Cairo, standing before him.

She told him about her husband's entanglement with the Mafia, which led to his imprisonment, and their separation. After that she had moved back to Italy and opened up an auction house, where she sold what she still had of her antique collections. Now she was trying to reestablish the business contacts she had had before her marriage.

He learned from her that Sabina had gotten married after her father, Signor Stirforti, had pushed her into a relationship with a relative of his who was an officer in the Italian navy. She left Rome and went to live with him in a town twenty miles from Pisa. She gave birth to a daughter, and had a nervous breakdown. On more than one occasion, she had tried to commit suicide, but she was now an outpatient at a mental health clinic, where she attended sessions to treat the depression that had overcome her. Her husband didn't visit her much, since he was often at sea. He also learned from her that her father had been struck by agoraphobia, which made him fear people and society, because of the guilt he felt for causing his daughter's condition.

Photography: Black and White

"I feel like I don't belong and it's killing me."

Thus had bitterness penetrated Sawsan's soul, and the language of complaint came to be her preferred lexicon. Salim was being held in prison and had been away for a long time. She visited him from time to time at the political prisoners' cellblock at Tura Prison. She could get there in an hour-and-a-half, leaving her house at nine o'clock and waiting for the microbus at Ramses Square. She would contemplate the statue of Ramses II standing upright, covered in dust and draped in grief for the state he had ended up in, here in this city square. If only the ancient Egyptians had known the fate that would meet their deified king, they would have plucked him off his throne and rued the day they had ever taken him for a god—a god they worshiped and granted the right of absolute power over their lives. She looked at him and wondered, *Was he really a god or was that just an ancient myth?* His slender body, his smooth stomach, his chin, the look in his eyes, his silent grandeur, the magnificence of one who is sure of himself and his authority among his followers. As the microbus passed by the tomb of Sidi Ibn al-Farid she remembered that pleasant evening when she went with Salim to celebrate the mulid of this saint, God's Familiar and Master of Sufis. There, verses of Sufi poetry were poured out, accompanied by music, and her body hummed along with the drumbeats and the steady rhythms of the participants in the zikr. She went down to the open space of the zikr and intoxication flowed over her. The sky began to fill her vision, as though there were a light within it that was drawing her toward it. She felt that she had grown light, hurling into endless space, and floating down like a feather. Her burdens were dropping away from her, the world was spinning around her, and Salim's eyes multiplied like crescent moons illuminating the sky. She felt that the state she was in was the most powerful in the universe. The universe drew her to its bosom and carried her in its arms. Her breaths were warm; she seized it by the hands and wished it would let her course through the tremors of its heart and the very pores of its soul, and create for her a world other than the one she was living in.

❖

I graduated from the university and began teaching French professionally, and I came to have a professional dossier on file with the Ministry of Education and Training. It contained my name and my mother's name, my address, my age, birthday, number of relatives and their places of employment, a statement on my financial liabilities, the number of properties I owned, and a list of assets I have in my possession—in case of future bribery and embezzlement —and six photos of me with a posed look on my face that the photographer had asked me to make. Government photos: they have to be miserable pictures to reflect the reality of the present; no laughter and no smiling. As though the world has to see you with a neutral expression, not marked by any emotion. As though you don't have the right to show them a different image. And an official police record that carried my fingerprints—prints that showed the grease left by all the people who took my hand to cross the street when I was a little girl, and the number of whacks of the cane that I received in school because I accidentally made a mistake, and all the dishes I've washed, and all the times I cut my fingers when I toyed with a razor without realizing the danger, and all the times my hands touched Salim's and I felt safe with him, and all the times I raised my hands to heaven in supplication.

My mother says that I've grown up, and that the time has come to get married, but who would I marry? I don't deny that I have my needs, but what's the use if the body is fulfilled but the spirit is lost? I want the spirit. The spirit will quench the body's thirst and satisfy it.

But how does a woman fulfill her needs if her spirit is tormented? If she marries a man she doesn't love while her spirit yearns for another. Isn't that a sin? Or does sin only happen when she has a relationship outside of marriage? How can she allow herself to be on intimate terms with someone she loathes? When she places her body beneath his and then hates herself for it, feeling disgusted by her own body odor that has mingled with his and made its way into her very core?

The last time I saw Salim he seemed oppressed and hopeless. I smiled at him to lighten the pain of his loneliness. I used to feel beautiful when I saw him looking at me. I would make a point of smiling, and bring him a packet of cigarettes, some magazines, some stories by Yusuf Idris that he likes so much. Sometimes I would joke with him, telling him, "You look fantastic in that blue uniform." His uniform was faded, his hair haphazardly cut, and his face pale, but despite all that, he was beautiful. Our hands touched through the iron bars and I melted.

As usual, I console him with a few trite sentences like, "Tomorrow you will get out of here, and you'll get a job, and you will realize all your hopes." But he always says that he will never leave this prison.

I contemplate the meaning of freedom: here I am, set free, and Salim is behind prison walls. Sadat announces that students who get involved in politics are corrupted because they aren't taking an interest in what they came to the university for. They are victims of alien thinking from countries that are hostile to us. Salim makes it clear that I shouldn't wait for him, and he urges me to find a relationship with someone else, but I don't want anyone but him. From a distance I notice the writing on the walls: "We will come back stronger than we were," "We will make Egypt Islamic." I see drawings of different weapons, and I tremble in fear. I leave the prison behind me, sad and depressed.

Although Sawsan had read in the newspapers that Sadat was releasing political detainees on the occasion of the

October 6th celebrations, Salim didn't leave prison. She was bored of studying and teaching. She began to write, and then send what she had written to the newspapers. She wanted to write about what was taking place inside her, about her apprehensions and fears, about her vision of reality and existence. She wanted to change reality, a reality that had become neglected through poverty, want, and subjugation. She would not use literature as a kind of catharsis for repressed emotions; instead, she would use it to give expression to the anxious, tormented spirit of humanity.

Her thoughts were always about Salim who had still not yet been released. Many times recently she had been to Tura Prison without being allowed to enter for security reasons. This time she would shout in their faces: she wouldn't sit there tongue-tied with her arms crossed. It was her right to see him even if only to tell him of her desire to be free of him and go on with her life.

This time, too, she couldn't go through with it. On her way back, she couldn't find a ride, so she was forced to walk along the road that cuts through the desert. She was afraid and wondered, *What if I die here? What if someone rapes me?* The heat was nearly suffocating her. Eventually, she noticed a military jeep from a distance. She signaled to it, as though she and the jeep had planned to meet. The driver stopped the car and the accompanying officer asked her to get in. He welcomed her with a smile and asked her where she was headed. She asked him to let her off at the closest place where she could continue her trip to the city. Then there was silence, which she broke by saying, "Praise God there's no war now. The peace treaty solved the problem."

"This peace is just on paper," he replied. "The army has other plans for it. We always have to be on our guard, and get ready to hit 'em with all we've got."

"But what about the economy and the cost of living?"

"That will take care of itself when the nation is strong, when it achieves military power and political influence."

The discussion, which she was happy to take part in, continued, and she forgot that she was in a military vehicle. They had good-natured Egyptian personalities, and when she told them about Said her feelings of isolation disappeared completely, and she felt a violent sense of kinship with them. She got out of the car while warmly thanking them and wishing them victory and success.

"We're here to protect you," one of them replied.

She walked far. She saw the muzzle of an artillery gun aimed toward her and in spite of everything, she felt herself shrivel up.

Semen

Here you are scratching the walls with your fingernails, making a calendar to mark the days you're spending in prison. You still have a lot more to go. It was your idealistic plans that brought you to this terrible state, deprived of seeing even a sunbeam of freedom or even thinking freely without feeling guilty.

Salim stared at the ceiling of his prison cell, remembering Sawsan. Desire was killing him: he recalled the dampness of the lecture-hall chairs during the cold winters, and the hoarseness of his voice the day after a well-attended rally. He remembered his family in the countryside: strong peasant men, and peasant women striking the fertile soil to draw out the goodness within it. He looked through the cell window with its four iron bars. He no longer had the strength to break this iron—he wasn't "David," only Salim, a young man. Wisdom hadn't endowed him with strength, and revolution hadn't granted him liberation; instead, he'd become an isolated prisoner, like Samson after his hair had been cut. He wasn't a victim of betrayal or conspiracy, but of blind power. Oh, if only he could shrink in size—then he could escape from these bars! Or, if he was a giant he could smash the walls. He hadn't seen the Nile for a long time. When he gets out, he will take a boat from Maadi to Aswan, and take Sawsan along with him. Just the two of them in the boat, to get away from this world. *Sawsan, I want to take you in my arms and draw my tormented body to your holy one. I want to quench my thirst in the wellsprings of your honey-brown eyes. To enter your world means heavenly bliss.*

"Lunch!" shouted the guard in an inhuman voice. He stretched out a hand covered in marks that reflected the years of brutishness and rough living he had spent in prison. Salim heard the sound of the peephole in the door closing shut, as though the world were dying. *Look at your food, no savory smell and the taste gone off it.* He stretched out his hand, and placed a crust of bread in his mouth. But his heart wasn't in it, and he lost the desire to eat. It was like something choking him, and he spat it out. Hot tears welled up in his eyes, and his situation weighed down on him. Seas of saltwater streams lapped against the shores of his lips. With his wrist, he wiped away his tears, and smelled the odor of his sweat. He savored it, and curled up in a fetal position, placing his hands between his thighs. With his very being, body and spirit, he concentrated on the moment of isolation, visualizing Sawsan and all the women of the world. Then he slept: the tear gas, the clamoring voices, the state security truncheons, and Sawsan's cries to her friend who had fallen amid the crowd all evaporated, and he savored the smell of semen in the secret places of lust and the body's surprising feebleness. He imagined children: girls and boys from this fluid flowing and splashing around him in his cell, creating an atmosphere of surging humanity, filled with noisy happiness and tears.

Salim, don't be like the wretched of the earth. Convictions are the essence of life! Do what you resolved to do, what you pledged yourself and your brothers to. The solution is escape. Carrying out the agreed-on plan is the natural conclusion to what you started.

Salim broke into a run, afraid and alone. His courage failed him: he couldn't look behind him and see his fellow escapees fall into the hands of the police or see the dogs snapping at their flesh. He fled Tura Prison the way Moses fled Pharaoh's city to Midian, but with the difference that Moses would be filled with light there at the mountain. As for Salim, the world grew dark around him until he reached Ihab al-Shinawi with his shoulder bleeding and his soul empty and extinguished.

Sawsan headed out downtown. She entered the lobby of the Hilton, and breathed in the clean, perfumed fragrance of the reception lounge. She passed through the lobby to the Nile, where small boats cut a path through the water, and where shadows and sun embraced beneath the Qasr al-Nil Bridge. She walked below the two stone lions that guard the bridge, and a memory of Said washed over her. Her eyes were bathed in tears that flowed warmly over her cheeks. She leaned on the railing, and her tears grew cold in the breeze.

She wandered about in the streets of Cairo, passing by the American University, across the street from the Mugamma with its labyrinth of cubicles. She sniffed the pleasant smell of coffee in the Ali Baba Café, and it reminded her of Salim and student meetings at the university coffee shop. An argument was breaking out with one of the Nasserists who didn't like all the nice talk about Sadat. He started talking about Nasser and Arab nationalism, until the whole thing came to blows, and she left. She heard the sound of a helicopter, and turned to look up at the sky. In her intense weariness, she wished she could ride in it. She crossed the square. Suddenly the flow of cars came to a halt, preventing pedestrians from crossing through the traffic barriers. The traffic-signals went dead and car-horns blared in protest.

It was an unusual day. . . . Things stayed like that for over an hour and a half, with no movement and no news. Sawsan heard a rumor that Sadat had been assassinated, and that something important had happened in Medinat Nasr. The sky over Tahrir Square was blocked by a cloud of dust and smoke. State security cars fanned out everywhere. There was confusion as frightened masses of humanity started moving. Everyone was wondering, "Who killed him?"

The alley was dressed in mourning and Sawsan noticed Budur pulling a black scarf over her head. "Even if our Lord takes His revenge on them," Budur told her, "the man is dead." Sawsan's mother cried a lot, more than she did the day Nasser died, and she felt the scar on her eyebrow, and didn't touch food for two days. She stopped asking about Said. "For sure he's dead," she said, "just like Sadat."

But she didn't accept the idea: "He'll come back tomorrow," she said. She sang Sharifa Fadil's song, "My dear son, light of my life!" she switched on the radio to the Qur'an broadcast all day long and drank black coffee. Sawsan asked herself about the new president: she liked his image on television and marveled at his voice and appearance, saying, "If Salim was here, he'd be arguing with me about this." She felt lonely and isolated, and couldn't go out in the late afternoon as she usually did in order to buy that day's *al-Ahram* newspaper. She eventually changed her mind, but Budur caught up with her at the end of the alley. She was barefoot. "You're crazy!" she told her. "You want to get arrested or something? There's a curfew, you know! Come with me, and stop acting so crazy."

In her room, Sawsan wondered whether Ihab al-Shinawi and Salim had anything to do with Sadat's assassination. Suddenly, the apartment in Bulaq and what had happened there popped up into her head, and the hair on the back of her neck stood up.

Days passed and the people of alley forgot about Sadat. They were delighted with the return of Egyptian territory. Budur and I were growing distant and I started to consider our different circumstances. I realized that Budur was the only one who fully comprehended the reality of the matter, that she was putting delusions aside and setting a goal for herself. Money was her focus; she was moving ahead for it, and it was never far from her thoughts when she woke up in the morning. When I met her recently, I spoke with her about Girgis. I was bothered by what was happening to him, and I considered it my obligation to turn her attention to it,

72

so that she wouldn't kill him with neglect. "Are you happy about what's happening with Girgis?" I asked her.

"What happened to *him*? *He's* the one who brought it on himself! Did someone tell him to neglect his work, drink himself senseless, and wander the streets like a fool?"

"Shouldn't you do something?"

"What do you want me to do? Should I leave my work and sit beside him in the alley with the half-dead people there?"

"Those people are good folk—they're not to blame. Strange things happen in life. No one chooses to be poor."

"But we can change from being poor to being rich!"

"Not everyone can do that."

"Good. Then they can keep their nose out of my business."

"I apologize if I've been forward. I just wanted to bring something important to your attention. If you lose Girgis, you won't find anyone else."

"What's your point? Luka is a good person. The only thing going on between him and me is work."

"Listen, Budur. I'm not comfortable about this Luka business, and in any case, I don't know him the way you do. I'm just telling you that Luka is looking out for himself first and foremost, just like everyone else these days."

"So if you already know that, then why are you giving me this lecture and blaming me?"

"Because you're my friend and my neighbor. You're my sister, too. I don't have anyone, Budur—just God and that's it. He's left my Mama for me, and you know her condition, and what she's like now. I've known you since I was born, Budur. We're like one person. You're a part of me—a part of my life—and your husband Girgis is like my brother."

"Your brother, huh?" Budur answered sarcastically. "Your brother in Islam?"

"Budur, what kind of new talk is this? Since when do we talk about religion—Islam this and Christianity that? We're sisters. Our God rules over our hearts: I swear, I've never felt that you were somehow different from me."

A tone of sadness came over Budur. I had known for a long time that her aunt died when extremist groups set fire to the tents of the mulid of St. George in one of the cities in Upper Egypt. She noticed that I hadn't blamed her for taking sides against me, but I told her, "The goal of extremist groups—whether Christian or Muslim—is to kill off the unity and love between us. We can't give them the opportunity. Let's stop this."

When Budur understood how I felt about her, she returned to her cheerful disposition again, and was completely honest and open with me. She told me about her relationship with Luka, her affection for Girgis, and, despite that, her desire to separate from him. I advised her to think about it, and discuss it with Girgis before taking any decision.

Within a few days, Budur's situation changed. She was no longer the same Christian girl who would go to church on Sunday to make her confession to the priest, and she stopped going to the doctors for fertility treatments. She now understood that she was infertile, and that she was incapable of growing new life in her womb. She abandoned her loyalty to Girgis and lived the other life she used to thirst after with all her being. Her infrequent visits to the alley began to make her nauseous, and whenever she entered it, she felt she was retreating into a squalid prison cell that struck her with a sense of terror, as though she had been sentenced to remain there forever—a narrow alley with broken-down houses, and people who lived below the poverty line and scrambled after crumbs. She felt fear and confusion as she walked through it, sensing their baleful looks. "No, things can't go on like this. I have to put an end to this torture. Separating from him is the solution—any solution is better than this split existence. Luka is my destiny."

She took Sawsan's advice and brought up the subject with Girgis. He didn't respond and left it up to her to broach the subject the way she had planned it out in her mind until she finished. Then there was a period of silence that made her sense menace, as though she were seeing him for the first time. She was filled with a real sense of disconnection from him and from herself after she poured out what was within her. She regarded him the way she would someone that she didn't know at all: his stubbly chin, his disheveled hair, the smell of beer wafting up from him, mixed with other unpleasant smells. She wondered to herself, *Did I really live here? Is this the Girgis I once hoped to sing for?*

Suddenly, a wave of convulsive laughter overcame him. "Are you done with your big speech? Now come over here and give me a squeeze like we used to do."

She felt both distress and compassion for him, like a rich woman who had noticed a beggar in the street, cast her eye over him, and then decided that he didn't deserve her charity. He couldn't comprehend the look she was giving him, and in his drunken state he thought she had returned to him, contrite and appreciative of his patience, goodness, and self-sacrifice in his love for her. He shrugged off everything she had said to him and considered it a kind of flirtatious rebuke. He continued laughing mindlessly, and repeatedly tried to draw her to him. She warded him off with a firmness that sobered him up and stunned him for several seconds. Then he went to the opposite extreme, becoming an enraged animal, and started beating her and calling her terrible names. He paid no attention to the neighbors' entreaties as they banged on the door. He wanted revenge for all the disgrace he had put up with, he wanted to wipe out the insinuations, the innuendoes, the contempt. He was trembling, and sweat poured freely over his face and onto his filthy shirt. Her screaming turned into a sob and a moan, and she was certain that the end was coming. It was inevitable and she succumbed to her fate, asking God for forgiveness for all the sins she had committed. She made her confession to Him and asked Him to let her die so she could be at peace.

The neighbors succeeded in breaking open the apartment door. They pounced on him and pulled her away from underneath him. They sat him down on the sofa and splashed water on him. Some moments passed and everyone heard a sound like the howl of an injured dog. It gradually grew louder and higher, and then turned into a fit of weeping and sad sobs: "Enough! Leave me be! It's nothing—please get out before I throw you out!"

The rescuers withdrew after he assured them that everything was fine and Budur asked them to show themselves out.

"Enough, Budur. You've forgotten Girgis. You forgot our plans and dreams, everything. And for what? A Jew? You're leaving me because of someone like that?"

"Girgis! I'm not going so I can think it over, or to think about you! I'm going so we can put things right between us. Listen, Girgis, you're a good and decent man, and I want to be level with you. I want you to stay the good man you've always been. But we've been leading separate lives up to now."

Silence prevailed, as though a powerful fear had enveloped the room in a climate of dread. But there was an attempt by Budur to let it all out and free herself from the feelings of longing growing within her, "We're no longer useful each other now."

"What does that mean, 'We're no longer useful to each other'?"

"It means we have to separate—we have to divorce."

"We can't divorce. Get yourself another religion."

"Girgis! I'm being serious! Enough—it's over. I've had it; I get nothing out of it. The best thing we can do is separate on good terms."

"You killed off 'good terms' when you left me."

"Don't change the subject! Leaving you was a result, not the cause of anything."

"You mean to tell me that Luka isn't the reason?"

"Exactly. Luka has nothing to do with it."

"You're lying to yourself. Or you're lying to me: of course Luka is the reason for what we're in now. He's the reason I lost you. He's the reason for my failure and my collapse. That Jew is the reason. He took you from me—he took everything."

"Luka didn't take anything from you. Have you forgotten? Luka's given us everything: can you tell me where the store and the house in your name came from? And the boutique I have now, where do you think that came from? Luka isn't to blame—don't project your problems onto him."

"Why are you defending him like this? Who's your husband, me or him? You've completely lost me—you aren't the Budur I married and used to know. You're like those women I used to know before I married you: you're still just trash."

She felt the insult, and wanted to defend herself, but because what Girgis was saying had an element of truth to it, she didn't object. But she responded with a voice filled with grief, "Girgis, there's no need for insults. I want a divorce."

"I won't divorce you. This is my life, Budur. What's this Luka got to do with me?"

They failed to reach a mutual understanding; instead, their feelings of loathing only deepened. She left him. A stubborn feeling of regret and despair filled her.

Girgis remained alone in his half-darkened room, looking at the sewing machine and shears—those shears that he had used for so long, working for Luka wholeheartedly and with complete dedication. He picked them up from off the sewing machine, and felt them in his hands. They were smooth and cold to the touch. The silver-plated coating was corroded a little along the sharpened edge, but they were still solid, heavy, and sharp. They had never let him down. He looked at the shears, *You will be my traveling companion on the road to revenge.*

Although Girgis wasn't educated enough to pass judgments about the Jewish race, he had an instinctive hatred for Jews: they were the ones who provoked Christ's death; they were Egypt's enemies; they were the ones who usurped the land of Palestine and disgraced the Holy Land. It was because of them that the best of his friends, relatives, and loved ones had been murdered in the war. And so his rage against Luka increased and drove him to seek revenge. Luka had enticed them with money and they had responded to it because they were poor. He knew how to tempt Girgis' wife and she gave in because she was seduced by his good life. He became convinced that if he killed Luka, Budur would come back to him the way she once was, a child with her eyes closed to the world, submissive and obedient.

The shears are the only way to get back what was stolen from me, what is mine by right. Luka robbed me of my wife, and I have to rob him of his life.

Sawsan

I advise the girls in my class to take their time choosing their partner, even if it means delaying marriage, so they don't make a mistake. Self-control is the way to happiness. Do I practice self-control myself? Sometimes when I leave the school, I'm like someone lost in thought: I don't know what I'm doing, I wander the streets, I take the tram all the way to the end of the line and then take it all the way back again. I sit in front of a man, observing him. I don't turn my gaze away from him. Our eyes meet, and warmth spreads within my body. He's sending his lewd messages to certain places.... When I return home, I regret that I didn't stick to my principles about virtue. Are these small things incompatible with the idea of virtue—these things that make my life, filled with deprivation, bearable? Am I being a hypocrite with my students?

I pray a lot and implore forgiveness. I ask God to drive away this devil hidden within my bosom. In the end, I'm no different from Budur or Hamdiya who eloped with her boyfriend, or Fayza whose body was burned before my eyes after she had been forced to marry a man much older than she was. Whenever I saw her daughter, I could smell the odor of her burned flesh. Why don't I end my life? "Would you die an unbeliever like Fayza?" my mother asks me. "Look, Fayza was poorer than you and ignorant." If death is not the solution, then why do I find myself tired of the pleasures of life? Why am I stern and withdrawn like this? We only live life once, so get going, Sawsan—live! Salim won't come back, Said won't come back, and my mother is finished. What are you crying over, the future or the ghost of the past?

Occasionally, Luka would go to the restaurant at the Greek Club. He used to like to sit there. He knew its patrons and the waitstaff. He didn't sit with anyone, but just hunkered down in one of the corners, poring over the newspapers with a glass of beer. He let a part of his attention take in the din of mingled voices that would flow over his ears from the great dining room, making a reverberation he loved. Sometimes he listened in on a bit of conversation, then lost its thread and went back to reading. Sometimes he heard people chatting in Greek and his face would brighten up behind the newspaper, as he shared in the laughter going on but kept it to himself.

He remembered the old lady, a friend of his mother, who lived in the same apartment building, although it had been a long time since he had last seen her. He remembered his mother who would often bring him along with her to this place, so she could meet her friends after hours. Her laughter would resonate in the big room, emitting warmth and joy. Sometimes, when the wine had got to her head a little, she would put her hand over her glass and stand up. Then she would begin a snatch from a sad song, and amid the acclaim of people egging her on, she would suddenly stop singing because she remembered some verses about the nation, by poets well-known or obscure, and she would light up the room with patriotic enthusiasm. One or two would get up and dance the Greek *hasapiko* to the strains of an unheard bouzouki.

In the past, he tried to write poetry but failed, in a notebook he had held on to for a long time. He wrote out verses to Sabina but hadn't read them to her:

> In ancient tales, they say
> That the princess with fabled hair
> Built for her true love a ladder to climb
> And at night she sits with him
> Conversing with the shy moon
> And they dance with the stars to the music
>   of existence
> This princess is you.

After she left, he loathed those lines, telling himself that they were mere words. He convinced himself that he was living poetry in his life, and that he was transforming his life into beautiful rhythmic poetry, that no poem in the world could sing what he was feeling when he rested his hands in Sabina's, clasped them, brought them to his lips, kissed the tips of her fingers, and passed his own over the skin of her dewy cheek. No poetry in existence could evoke for him his painful longing to touch her when she came into view a few steps away from him. It was then that he suffered from an excess of happiness and hastened to span the distance of space and time between them.

He stood up and was heading for the door when he spotted Sawsan through the window crossing the street.

He remembered her instantly since she hadn't changed much: the same innocent face, the same restive pace, the same fabled hair that had impressed him when he saw her with Budur that time. He imagined her as an eastern princess in exile, riding a white steed, and letting her hair fly in the wind as the horse galloped through green fields beside an endless shore.

He picked her out from among the crowd, and she was quite surprised to see him. Despite the blush that came to her face, she immediately felt a degree of closeness to him, because she had come to know him well through Budur. He invited her to Groppi's and she didn't hesitate. Her voice was soft, like Sabina's was, and a hidden joy crept into his heart that brought him back to the imagined world he had been in a few moments before. He wished he could just let her talk while he kept on listening to her pleasant voice.

The conversation began, naturally enough, with talk about Budur, but soon enough it turned to Luka and Sawsan, about their lives, feelings, and dreams. He let himself talk about the Jews and their plight, about his mother and father. For her part she poured herself out and revealed to him her relationship with Salim, and his intellectual crisis that had led him to prison. Their conversation grew long and they would have to meet again to finish it. They made plans to meet again at the Nile Hilton. He paid the bill and left.

She remained seated, looking serious. She couldn't believe what had happened: just now, and without much to-do, she had agreed to meet her friend's boyfriend. *Sawsan, you're wicked! How could you believe his sweet talk! He's a ladies' man—you know that! How could you let yourself be fooled?* She bit her lip. *But that can't be what he is. This is the same Luka that Budur talks about. He's well read, knowledgeable, and reasonable. He speaks candidly and frankly about everything. There's a big difference between him and Budur.*

When she was talking with him, she felt that she was speaking with a voice not her own, and expressing opinions she didn't believe in. She found herself enthusiastically defending the peace initiative, the rejection of disputes, tolerance among peoples, and the right of the Jews to live their lives. She found herself a humanist in the extreme, and forgot about massacres and wars. She forgot about her dead brother and her mother's grief and Salim locked up behind bars. She forgot about Budur and Girgis and the people of the alley, *"It doesn't concern me. Isn't sinning part of the chemical makeup of humanity? Didn't Budur say that she wasn't bothered by what others said about her, and that she's doing what she wants? Why don't I do what I want, too? She didn't take into account Girgis' feelings and trampled all over them without remorse. If I treated her the same way, would I be wrong?*

On the way home, she saw Girgis squatting, talking to himself, and spitting on the ground in a revolting manner. He was raving, saying strange words, as though he were arguing his case to someone. In front of him sat a man who seemed near death's door. He was holding a rusty needle and pricking the shape of a cross into Girgis' wrist. She was afraid, but she approached him and said hello. He didn't respond, but just kept talking to himself. She patted his shoulder and reminded him who she was. He didn't look up except when she mentioned Budur's name. He seemed to wake up at that, and asked her, "Where is Budur? She didn't leave— the Jew took her from me. . . . That's why I'm getting the cross tattoo again, so when I die they'll know I'm a

Christian, not a Jew." He returned to his waking state for a moment, remembered who Sawsan was, and burst into heavy sobs. Then he withdrew once again into the dark recesses of his diseased mind, and began to threaten Luka with dire consequences.

He clutched his neck with his dirt-covered hand and said, "Life without Budur is death. He's a dead man now, and Budur is dead. Only blood will bring them back to life."

Sawsan was extremely alarmed by Girgis' ravings, since hearing Luka's name had come to have a different effect on her. Feeling mean-spirited in spite of herself, she took Girgis' hand and lifted him from where he was sitting and asked him politely, pleading with him, to come with her to her house, because al-Hajja, her mother, was asking about him and wanted to see him. "Get up, and come with me, Girgis. I'll bring Budur to you. I know she's not well. But everything will be all right: she'll come back to you . . . ."

Her words were soothing, calming his temper, and he acquiesced, letting her lead him to her house.

She's stubborn in her affection and insistent on it, Luka told himself. *She believes it's as real as she is. If I hadn't given in to her, then that would have been the end of it, but it's high time I got over her. We're not a good fit at all, and we were only together because we were needy and weak. If I were free of her,* he wondered, *and she were free of me, would her relationship with Girgis go back to what it was?*

Luka didn't try asking her whether she loved Girgis or not. And he didn't try asking her why she loved him, since Girgis' naivete and meekness worried him. Sometimes he got the sneaking feeling there was a conspiratorial connivance between Girgis and Budur.

Sawsan had a lot of terrible dreams, but recently they had begun to emerge, involuntarily, into the waking world. Often she imagined and dreamed about Luka each time after she met Budur, who didn't hold back from telling her everything. One day, Budur forgot that she was talking with a young unmarried woman, and related to her in full detail an entire night she had spent with Luka. Sawsan didn't sleep that night, she kept remembering Budur's words and imagining her again and again. In her troubling dream, she imagined Luka coming to her after Budur's unexpected death, as she embraced him in her arms, and guided him to the secrets of her body. Then Salim appeared before her, completely naked, and hanging from a pink noose, which instantly turned into a snake that opened its mouth to bite her and swallow her up completely. Sawsan woke up when her mother gave her a strong shake on the shoulder, "I seek refuge in God from that accursed Satan! Wake up, dear. Who were you talking to?"

To live with and overcome her obsession, Sawsan tried to throw herself into her work, continuing the project she had started on her own to develop a French-language teaching course. She wanted to rid French lessons of conventional phrases that were no longer used in daily life. She discussed the subject with both the head teacher and the general supervisor, but despite their show of approval, the idea met with rejection on the grounds that the ministry was more concerned about her lack of experience and her ability to develop the program: there was no objection to someone bringing the matter up with their superiors to get their opinion, but *pay attention, Mademoiselle, to your studies: exams are right around the corner, and you're wasting time with inappropriate ideas like these.*

The Departure

Luka gave serious thought to leaving Egypt, especially after Sadat's assassination. Sawsan hadn't been able to convince him of the sincerity of her beliefs—her new ones concerning the Jews. Although he had read other things between the lines of what she was saying that confirmed for him how much affection they had for each other, day after day, how could he brush away the cruel effects Israel was having on the defenseless people of Palestine?

—Wouldn't it be better for me to go to Israel and work with the Jewish groups there demanding peace? If I truly love Egypt, then I can serve it from there. But no, Israel is a fantasy and a mirage, so let me go to Italy and look for Sabina, so we can pick up where we left off. I feel certain that she is waiting for me, and that she'll leave her husband. Together, we'll go to the ends of the earth and live our lives. I'll sell all I have here and buy us a house in Greece overlooking the Gulf of Corinth in the south, or Macedonia in the north, or anywhere she likes. I've got nothing left except emptiness. Budur has become awful: her love is a new prison called conscience. And now, Sawsan—no, no, I can't—I'm putting an end to the role I've been assigned here. Life is just a joke and idle chitchat, and then you go to hell.

Sawsan wrote in her notebook, "The alley I live in hasn't changed since I was a small child. The same kindly faces, the same glances that follow passers-by with curiosity and bemusement. The world is changing outside—wars and catastrophes are going on—but the alley is the same as always. Nothing changes in it. Even the mud brick has become as faded as it's going to be: perhaps it will fade even further, but only grudgingly. Houses get painted, but their color dies out quickly and they go back to being just like the rest of the alley. The dust can never kill this alley off. I feel like a foreigner among people there, and I've grown distant from them. But I know them well: sometimes I've given up on them, but I don't hate them. I aspire to a world where your clothes, your identity, and your class aren't boxed in. I want to live in a world where I can mention my place of birth without arousing any kind of prejudice against me. My mother says the alley is the world she knows, and she doesn't care to know any other. There was no one left in the alley: all her old friends had moved away and changed. The only ones who remained were either stuck in their ways or else time had passed them by, like the withered leaves of autumn that cry out in pain when our feet trample over them to remind us of their reality and ours."

One sunny day, Girgis went where his inclination took him. He climbed the staircase his feet remembered well, and knocked on the door, which Budur's mother opened up to him. A frown appeared on her face.

"So you've come—the man of the house!" She accused him of being weak and feeble, telling him that his manhood was gone and had shriveled up inside him, that his wife was in charge now, and that he had no role in life anymore. Then she grew more vehement, telling him that she didn't want to see his face unless he was with Budur, and that if he wasn't capable of being a man and keeping people's tongues from wagging, so she could hold her head high in the alley, then she would ask her brother to support them instead. After she'd poured out her invective, he got up, left, and said nothing.

Luka tried to avoid Budur, since he had made up his mind to stay away from her. When these attempts failed, he decided to disappear from Cairo. In vain she tried to reach him, and when she was unsuccessful, she wrote to him:

> Luka,
> I'm afraid for you. Girgis has become like a crazy man—loneliness has robbed him of his right mind. The only thing he wants is to take revenge on you. Don't stay in Cairo. I'm going to Alexandria: I'll come see you there.
> Your darling forever,
> Budur

> Luka,
> I haven't found you in any of the places I know. Did you get my last letter? I don't want to lose you. Life is just you and being with you. I don't want anything else from the world except to be by your side. I've been looking for you everywhere. I can't imagine the world without you. If you were to die now while I was by your side, then I would have had everything I wanted from the world. But I don't want you to die and I don't want to die

because I want you beside me. I'll tell you again:
Cairo has become dangerous for you. Get out as
quickly as possible.
Budur

She felt that her life had come to a halt. She wanted to get
through to him by any means. She thought about going to
Sawsan, but how could she, since she had cut off relations
with her such a long time ago? Why is she clinging to him like
this? She should accept her fate and let him go. At the end of
the day, he is Jewish, and there is no one for her but Girgis,
who she wed in holy matrimony. No one will consider what
she's doing acceptable and she will be left to wander alone
in the world. Why did she write to him, instead of leaving him
to meet his fate? *Christ had suffered and bore the cross on his
shoulders, and now I'm in love with a descendant of Judas.* Or so
she convinced herself to calm herself down.

Prayer of the Candles

Luka didn't answer Budur's letters, since his feelings for
her had died out, but she insisted on seeing him. Their final
meeting was marked by coldness and awkwardness on his
part, despite persistent attempts through her eager body
language to assure herself that he hadn't changed, and that
the lukewarm feeling she was getting from him didn't mean
anything. After their bodies had cooled down, he looked at
her fleshy torso, her hair mingled with sweat, spread out over
her neck and forehead, her lifeless, spent thighs, with tiny
sprouting hairs appearing on them. As for him, he seemed
old and gray to her. Wrinkles appeared on his face and chest,

and Budur saw him as the old, gray-haired man he essentially was. She felt a lump in her throat, and she was suddenly struck with self-loathing. She recalled her sins, and the Virgin appeared to her and chastised her. She beheld heaven behind the angry veils, and heard the voice of the Lord reminding her of punishments, and commanding her to return unconditionally to Him, or else eternal damnation would be her fate.

She got dressed and picked up her handbag. Feeling weary and overwhelmed, she didn't turn toward Luka, and avoided looking at him. She didn't want to hate herself more than she already did—she was as guilty as he was, in any case. She went out into the street, slapped her face, and was struck by an overwhelming desire to vomit. She hurried to the beachfront, and her stomach heaved, emptying out in successive waves everything that was inside her. Nothing was left except a bitter taste and pain. She looked at the sea-foam crashing over the waves and the endless horizon and wept. *Budur, you're ruined. Everything you were afraid would happen this whole time has happened.* She walked along the Corniche like a mad woman. From a distance she saw the darkness of the sea taking form in fearful shapes. The image of her as a small child standing in front of Lake Qarun came back to her; then she imagined her grand-mother emerging from the water, carrying on her head a chest inlaid with golden serpent-heads. Her grandmother places it in front of her, opens it, lies Budur down in it, and closes it on her.

She woke up out of her reverie, to find herself bumping against the shoulders of passersby. A car had almost struck her, and some compassionate soul took pity on her and brought her to the taxi stand. The whole way back to Cairo, she had her eyes closed and saw neither houses nor streets, and she cast off the curse of the waters. When the taxi let her out on al-Tura Street in Bulaq, she didn't know how much time had passed since she'd left Luka's house.

She passed by Shaban Street, then Aziz Khalil, then al-Hafiziya, then Bahr al-Qaraqol al-Bahri and ended up on Shubra's main street. It was already dark, and some dim lights glowed weakly through open windows. Several times her feet stumbled on a cobblestone as she walked along the church's railing, her whole body groaning, *Have you not thought about our Lord?* She found herself facing the large doors, as though Saint Theresa were summoning her to hurry up. She felt like her strength was leaving her, as though she were looking into the bottom of a deep grave. An image of herself as a small child appeared before her: she was playing and enjoying herself in the church courtyard. She saw the statue of the Virgin standing tall in the entryway, a statue of marble mounted on a pedestal covered with flowers. It appeared pale and sad in the nighttime light. She bowed her head in submission and hurried inside.

Here was her beginning, and here she would come when she died. Here she had been baptized and immersed in holy water. Here she had been married and here was where she used to find comfort. Why had she angered God, the Virgin, Saint Theresa and all the saints? *How can I find salvation, Saint Theresa? You found your path to it, when you were twenty-four. You relieved yourself of the burden of life, you became a nun and served Him until your pure soul left your body. You were my ideal once. What would I be without you? Chaste Saint Theresa, take me by the hand.*

She went down into the vault below, descending three steps. The tomb was cold, and the lit candles around it gave off no heat. Within lay the relics of Saint Theresa, peaceful and angelic. Her profound silence called on all humanity to cast off sin and repent. She heard her say, *Now, Budur, come to me.*

She headed toward the spot for votive offerings and prayed the Prayer of the Candles, murmuring, "May this flame burn away my sin, as the candle is burned by these flames."

The priest approached her. "Pray, Budur," he said.

She couldn't speak so he murmured in a soft voice filled with humility, placing his hand on her warm brow, and said, "Our Father, Who art in heaven, hallowed be Thy name. Thy Kingdom come, Thy will be done, on earth as it is in heaven . . . . Forgive us our trespasses, as we forgive those who trespass against us. And lead us not in temptation, but deliver us from evil. For Thine is the kingdom, and the power, and the glory, forever and ever. Amen."

She found herself unable to repeat what the priest was saying, and wept as she never had before. Her tears fell copiously, like a gushing wellspring that waters the desert of a soul thirsty for forgiveness. Through her dazzled eyes, she saw the icons start to move and beheld the saints hovering around her. They were looking down on her with sympathy and affection. The walls began to spin and the ground to move in waves beneath her feet and she fell down, unconscious.

❖

Girgis hadn't had a restful sleep in four straight days: he was thinking about his plan for revenge, and how he would blot out the disgrace that had clung to him for so long. He observed Luka from up close, but couldn't work out a precise plan for it, because Luka's circumstances had been chaotic in recent days. He chose the garage as a place to meet him, and showed up unexpectedly. He greeted him with a phony affection, but couldn't conceal the violent look in his eyes. Luka gave him a tepid greeting, and had him sit down beside him in the car as they used to do in times past. Neither one asked the other were he was headed, and the car set off onto the street with no particular destination. Luka tried to fill the terrifying empty space that had settled between them by telling him all the details of his life and his crisis about leaving Egypt, since his life had become meaningless and things were now all the same to him: work and rest, love and hate, life and death.

Luka found himself heading toward Pyramids Road, which they both knew well, but this time it seemed as though they were seeing everything for the first time: closed bazaars and amusement halls, a few pedestrians, and a traffic policeman in a black uniform who stood gesticulating on the traffic island. Although it was October, the sun was intensely bright. The car got as far as the incline at the foot of the pyramids, and made its way around the roundabout from the east side, coming to a halt at a rocky hill. They sat in silence. Luka took out a packet of Gauloises and offered one to Girgis. There was a half-smile on Girgis' lips as he closed them tightly on the cigarette that he always accepted from Luka, even though he didn't smoke.

"Girgis, I know you're keeping quiet about something."

Girgis took several puffs in succession on the cigarette, and then burst out of the car, roaring at Luka to get out. In a matter of seconds, they were grappling with each other in a vicious fight. They fell to the ground and rolled downhill. The tailor's shears fell out of Girgis' pocket. He ran over to them, and before Luka could recover from the effect of the fall, he found Girgis rushing toward him, brandishing his shears. He tried to deflect the blow, but streams of warm blood flowed from between his fingers. The sight of blood only increased Girgis' madness. "I killed him! I killed him!" he shouted, laughing. "I've washed away my dishonor! It's all over, Budur—no Jew will come between us! The Jew is dead! The Jew is dead!" He climbed the hill looking for someone to share this great news with, but saw only the desert sands, and heard only his voice echoing back from the rocks. He kept running, fell down, and got up more than once, not noticing the injuries and bruises that covered his face and body, or his clothes that had become filthy tatters. He came down the hill toward the Mena House Hotel, and came upon the security guards who grabbed hold of him to keep him from entering the hotel lobby, as he kept repeating his loud ravings.

The Apparition of the Virgin

Sawsan stood for a whole hour in front of the prison gate waiting for permission to enter. The heat was strong, the air was suffocating, and the Helwan factories nearby were churning out tons of industrial cement waste into the sky. Black-clothed mothers and fathers and old men with pale faces drained of color. Shouting and wailing.

The guard finally let her in to see the prison warden. He was polite and calmly asked her how close she was to Salim. Embarrassed, she told him that they were friends from their university days and as good as engaged. He smiled meaningfully and made no comment, but advised her, like a father would, to stay away from him.

"Salim has escaped, miss. But where can he go? We know everything about him and his group."

She didn't get over the shock until she was sitting in the microbus on the way back to Cairo.

—Salim did it. He longed to free himself from the prison of indecision and loss. And now he's found a way—but what way? It's my terrible fate. Said and my mother, and then Budur and Girgis, and now him. Who am I living for?

Daytime

In front of the Church of Saint Theresa, Sawsan suddenly comes upon enormous crowds of people circling around it, their eyes fixed on its high steeple. She asks what has happened and receives cryptic answers about an apparition of the Virgin there that evening, following yesterday's appearance at St. Mark's Church. She stands confused among the crowds, thinking about Salim and hoping he will return. She sees Budur squeezed amid the crowds, her gaze wandering and her movements hesitant, as though she were mounting a heaving wave. Sawsan tries to reach her, but can't. She loses her for a few moments amid the crowds, and then sees her as clear as sunlight. She tries to get close to her but fails. When she spots her, she is glad, but is astonished to see her swelling stomach. Their eyes meet, and everything that had come between them melts away amid the throngs. Budur lowers her eyes. Sawsan tries to stretch her hands out to her, but the flood of humanity is too fast for her, and she is lost in the crush.

Nighttime

Sawsan stands beside the al-Sahel police station, facing a state security car. Soldiers are pushing into it bearded men reciting aloud, "*Allahu akbar, Allahu akbar!*" She looks at them, contemplating their faces behind the windows with iron bars. Maybe Salim is among them. She feels pained and leaves. The tram quickly speeds by, frightening her, and her bracelet falls between its wheels. She leans over, picks it up, and keeps walking, passing by the Khazandar Mosque as the call to evening prayer goes out. She stares up at the sky and whispers a wish, casting it up toward heaven. The angels catch it and bear it aloft, up there.

Sleeping with Strangers

To Khalid and Abdelmegid, my brothers,
with great affection

Boston, Massachusetts: The Mid-1990s

Nadir went to the refrigerator, got out a bottle of cold water, and drank it almost to the bottom. He hated feeling full, believing that it was a sensation for the foolish and the rich, since it could prevent him from feeling attachment to others. The weather was hot and stifling, despite what they said about Massachusetts being one of the cold states, even in summer. Because it was located in the northern part of America, he told himself that perhaps the reason he felt so hot was the close quarters of the apartment he'd been living in for the last few days with his cousin Basim. Basim had come here several years ago with Jackie, the American girl he'd gotten to know in the Zahrat al-Bustan coffeeshop downtown. He had left university before completing his studies.

Nadir had missed Basim very much and was eager to visit him, because, of all his cousins, Basim was closest to him. The two of them agreed on everything, especially their love for music and singing. Basim welcomed him in historic Harvard Square, as they had agreed by phone. Basim was late, so Nadir was able to spend some time watching passersby at the Au Bon Pain café. He enjoyed talking to the artists and chess players who sat there for hours. It reminded him of his friend Hazim who was a chess addict: he never left the game, except to work as a trainer at one of the gyms in Sharm al-Sheikh.

The woman who got out of the car and was holding on to Basim's arm had Asian features. Nadir didn't ask him about Jackie. At first, Nadir didn't recognize Basim, since he had lost weight and grown a mustache. His clothes were unusual—he was wearing jeans and a sleeveless shirt—and he was driving a sleek-looking car. He said hello to Nadir and introduced him to Shuki. She was from Japan and was studying cosmetology in America.

"There's no time to lose," Basim said. "Get in."

The car took off, then came to a stop in front of a large building. "I'll wash the sweat and grime of Vermont off of you," said Basim. "We'll go to the sauna. I think you need it, after studying for a full year in a hick state like that."

At the sauna, Nadir took off his clothes, stripping himself of everything, even those that covered his private parts. He was shy about his body, like Adam the moment he first slept with Eve. In the steam room, men and women were sitting naked; the room was packed and the steam was thick enough to obscure vision completely. It almost suffocated him, and would have, had he not gotten out quickly to be hit by cool air. Basim pointed him toward the cold bath, which he got into. He found himself next to a man and woman who were flirting and fondling each other. Their private parts were out in the open, and hard to miss. He averted his eyes.

❖

The car drove along the Charles River, where trees were planted close together on each bank. The old buildings and towers reminded him of the enchanting Nile.

"This is where life is—not Vermont," Basim said, as he drove the car, turning to look at Nadir from time to time. "Boston is the oldest city in America. Once America was discovered, the English immigrated here, and then it became the homeland of the Irish. There's all nationalities here."

"Why don't you stay in Boston?" he added. "Studying at Harvard is where the future is. If it's a question of cost, arranging that is no problem." Then he turned on the car's cassette player to the song that goes: *Faraway mountain, my love lies beyond you.* At that moment, the voice of Fairuz blended naturally with his, creating an alluring, bucolic atmosphere. Nadir was lost in the high mountains, recalling Vermont and his two friends Sarah and Afaf, and the idea of writing a story came to him.

❖

My name is Nadir, and I had come to Vermont to study American literature. I had been feeling dissatisfied in Vermont. The girl I wanted to get close to there turned out to be a little strange: she preferred to be alone rather than with others. She did a lot of reading, and was always staring at people's faces, enthusiastically chatting with strangers, then dropping them, just like that. Despite my infatuation with her, I felt that she was afraid of sharing her life with someone else. I pictured her as a character in a novel, but not just an ordinary one, since she was full of contradictions. My frustration with her drove me to travel, so I left Vermont to visit Basim. Now here I am sitting with people who are completely alien to me, especially this Japanese woman with narrow eyes, and pallid, sallow skin.

"Shuki will be staying with us for two days," Basim assured me. "Then she'll leave, and you can relax."

The Japanese girl was very annoyed, as though another woman had taken her place.

"Don't worry about her. She'll be cool by tonight."

In the small apartment, which was in the neighborhood called Brighton, he offered me a drink, saying, "I'm sure you're going crazy for some Egyptian food." He ordered a takeout meal from a Lebanese restaurant, consisting of a plate of kofta, kebab, and rice pilaf.

"The U.S. is nothing at all like Egypt. You'll find everything you could ever dream of here. Try it and see: even if you don't have cash on you, you'll find that credit cards open up everything for you. Ask for it, and pay what you owe at your convenience."

In the evening, some Sudanese fellows came over and cooked a meal that filled the apartment with a strange smell, as if they had put all the spices of the east in the food. They sang a lot, and danced even more.

"These people are more sincere and loyal than any other nationality in the world," Basim said, as he sang an old tune along with them. Then they called it a night.

When we turned in, the girl was lying on the edge of the bed. I was next to the wall, and Basim was in the middle. I told him this was the first time I had slept in a bed with a woman who wasn't my mother or my sister.

Basim replied, as he roughly embraced and kissed her, "All humanity are brothers."

In the morning, the Japanese woman fought with him. When I asked him why they were fighting, he told me it was because we were talking in Arabic and she didn't understand the language. That's what infuriated her. She turned her face away, and her eyes went blank and grew narrower. I heard his voice get louder as he threatened her, "I escaped trouble in Egypt, so don't act like my jailer over here! I came here to be free, so I can be me, not what other people want. This is my cousin: he's a lot more important than you are. You should show him some respect!"

She cursed under her breath.

An hour later, the girl packed her bag and left. We sat down together.

"Women won't boss me around. She'll be back one day. Japanese women aren't a hot commodity here. American men love Spanish or Italian women—they love the spirit those women have, the spirit the men have lost themselves."

The apartment was now ours to kick back in: we watched television, cooked some food, and drank coffee. Then he started talking about his ex-wife, who had dragged him to court and took all the money he'd saved because he had slapped her when she refused to go along with his traditions, and told her she was a "whore who only wants men in her arms and between her legs."

"She got what she wanted once I arrived here," he said. "Now I'm working as a cab driver, and making good money."

"And what about learning, and the university, and singing?" I asked.

He made a rude hand gesture, and in a serious voice added, "Women love money and a good time."

Then he grabbed his guitar and began to strum the opening notes of the song "Try to Remember Me" by Abd al-Halim Hafez.

Suddenly, the phone rang, and he began talking with a girl in English. I thought it was Shuki, since he was telling her, "Calm down and come back: I'm waiting for you." Then he put the phone down and laughed.

"You're in luck, Nadir old man!" he said. "There's a real beauty about to come visit us: she's my buddy's girlfriend— Russian, and what a beauty! This chick is a runway model. She'll be here in a half hour. I told her I hate going behind someone's back, and she laughed."

"Russians are clever people," I said. "They helped us build the High Dam."

Olga was tall, slim, tanned, and gray-eyed, with golden hair that poured freely down the shaft of her slender neck.

She sat down quietly, and then the tears began to flow. She began sobbing loudly and Basim went up to her and took her in his arms. She rested comfortably on his shoulders, and after a little while, she sat up straight again. I handed her a Kleenex, and she thanked me.

"The bastard treats me badly and accuses me of doing awful things. He beats me up for cash and takes my money —the no-good, low-class. . . ." Then she drew back her skirt to reveal her thighs.

"He suspects I'm sleeping with another man," she went on, "because of these red welts and purple bruises. But I swear to Christ they're the fingerprints left by the angels that toss me around in my bad dreams all night long, ever since I've lived with him."

The Bob Marley song "No Woman No Cry" filled the empty space of the room, and when she listened to the final notes, the sound of her tears grew louder, so I tried to calm her down.

"Why don't you leave him?" I asked her, taking pity on her on account of the bruises and angel finger marks.

"I love him. I can't be away from him." Then she grew quiet, and said, "Who would I go to? I don't know anyone in this city, but I did know love from the touch of his hands. I tasted desire at the brush of his lips. I drank from the fountains of pleasure in his arms, and from the scent of his body that poured over me." Then she was quiet for a little while as she wiped away her tears. "But now I've got no use for him," she added, looking at me. "He's left me for an American actress, some unknown he seems to have fallen for. He spends the night with her, and doesn't come anywhere near me. The times we spend together now are just one long fight."

Suddenly the phone rang.

I heard him say, "So you won't put off coming until tomorrow, George?" I saw a look of nervousness on his face. Then he put the receiver down and said, "Olga ought to make herself scarce right about now. Her fiancé George will be here shortly."

"He mustn't see me here," she whispered in terror. "We'll have a fight, and he'll hit me." Her nervousness and fear infected me. I felt that she belonged to me and was mine alone, and that she was asking for my assistance. In my naivete, I imagined that this George person would argue with Basim and maybe a fistfight would break out between them, and all hell would break loose. With one hand I took her suitcase, and with the other I took her by the hand. It was cold and thin and I could feel the throbbing in her veins, transmitting signals to my entire body, so I quickened my steps. On the wooden steps leading to the roof of the building, the air was cold. The stars were bashful this evening, but they sent out a glimmer from time to time.

I sat her down beside the wall.

"Don't be afraid," I told her.

"The Great Escape," she replied.

At that moment I had a sense of my own importance. I snuck down the stairs, my heartbeats struck against each other in fear, and my pulse raced. As I touched the staircase walls, I felt again the touch of her hand, and the signals her hands had sent me a few minutes ago grew more insistent.

George was an ugly character, a shadow of the remnants of a man: tall, without a lot of hair, lean muscles revealed by the black, short-sleeved shirt that didn't fit him. He had an unnaturally prominent Adam's apple on his neck that provoked in me a desire to pluck it off and toss it at my feet. I listened to him talking about himself in a self-deluded, bitter way, like an old, beaten boxer threatening to defeat a young world champion in a rematch.

George talked about the women who chased after him everywhere, about loving the American girl who gave him everything—her money and her body—that he needed, and about his girlfriend Olga, and how he had discovered that she was cheating on him; and that he was the one who had given her the opportunity to come to America to work in the modeling business. How he had done it for her and for other girls with his photos that brought them to the attention of the most important fashion houses.

"Why do we always accuse a woman of being a prostitute if she gives her body to men who pay for it, but we don't talk at all about men who give themselves to women without expecting anything from them in return?" I asked Basim.

"You mean gigolos," he replied, as he made tea. "There's no need to be rude like that," he added, muttering under his breath. Then he sat next to George and nervously lit a cigarette.

But the thing that got me worried again was that George didn't ask about his missing girlfriend, not even once: wasn't he interested in finding out where she was? He didn't wander about—despite our nervous confusion when he arrived—in the studio apartment. He didn't trouble himself even to ask whether his girlfriend had called or not, and he didn't talk about her disappearance.

After he left the building at five in the morning, I went upstairs to her, carrying a flashlight in my hand, to ask her to come down: the danger was gone, and her cheating boyfriend had left. The cassette was on, replaying the same song over and over again. I made her an omelet, and gave her some bread and some apples. She ate like a refugee fleeing a famine. The tears flowed again. "You're very kind," she told me.

I laughed. "It's not what you think."

When she went to sleep, I asked Basim, "Aren't you going to sleep with her?"

"Not now," he said. "For the time being, she's my guest. But maybe it will happen. I don't know."

"Did you give her the address before she came to you?"

"No."

"And she's never come to visit you with this friend of hers, George?"

"Never."

"So how did she know how to get here?"

We looked at each other and laughed until there were tears in our eyes. Then we went to sleep next to her, just like with the last girl.

❖

The days Nadir spent with Basim didn't allow him to get to know this Olga woman: was there some secret agreement among them that involved her staying at Basim's while her penniless, unemployed boyfriend George knew all about it, so that Basim would take responsibility for her for a certain amount of time? Russians in America are looked on with some suspicion, even after the end of the Cold War: they live like secret agents who have to keep out of sight, and behave like parasites who have to be flicked off so they can learn to fend for themselves.

Since Olga set foot in the house, the smell of blue smoke lingered over it, to the point that I became addicted to the scent. As for the marijuana plants, they had spread out in the nooks and crannies of the house, like indoor plants. Basim was an expert at rolling joints, as if he were a local from Batniya, a veteran expert in the world of drugs. When I asked him what he got out of it, he said, "Life is sex, drugs, and music—like everyone used to believe in the sixties." During the day, Olga spent her time looking for a talent

110

agent, so she could work in the movies or in fashion, but the only offer she found was as a stripper at a nightclub. Basim didn't object to any work she took on.

When I asked, "But even if her job requires her to be naked in front of people?" Basim replied, "She is free and she's an adult. There are no legal guardians looking over anyone: it's a world where everything's out in the open, not schizophrenic, like in Egypt."

My vacation came to an end, and Basim came with me to buy me some presents, but his credit card wasn't working—or, to put it another way, he had maxed out his credit limit. We wandered around again in one of the stores and he took a T-shirt off one of the racks. He put it on and pulled off the security tag. When we left the store, he took it off and gave it to me. We embraced.

"You have to take back something new with you to Egypt," he said. "I don't want you to go," he added. "Stay here. You're going back to misery and dust, where people are treated carelessly like they're unwanted animals, and where dignity is crushed. Better to live here in a dump than go back to a country that doesn't respect its people."

"We should be blaming people, not the country," I replied. "We want to better ourselves. If all the good people left Egypt, who would be left there? Your fate is tied to your nation's."

"Spare me the useless speeches," he said. "Be practical—no one cares about any of that. Stick with me and we'll realize the American dream together."

The bus was ready to depart. I said goodbye to him, pretending not to care so much about him, as I fled the painful moment of separation. I got on the bus. On the other side of the glass, rain came down in torrents, falling on his face like tears. When the bus started moving, I noticed him crossing the street. Olga was waiting for him on the other side.

Cairo: The Late 1990s

Basim was deported after he left Hillsborough County Jail in New Hampshire. He was handed over to Egyptian authorities, which was a big shock to me, since I had always believed that Basim was smart enough not to get involved in any activity that would land him in prison, or would bring him into conflict with the authorities in any way. But it happened after he had failed to pay alimony fees the court had ordered him to pay his ex-wife Jackie. The complaints from his girlfriends grew more numerous—that he hit them and kicked them out for good, and above all, that he had an excessive love for drugs, especially hashish.

At the police station, where his father, my brother, and I went to get him, he was broken and pale, as though he had been sick for a year. Although his father's clout had led to the drug charges being dropped, the illegal residency in the U.S. was the main charge leveled at him. Later, those charges were dropped when he was deported to Egypt, and so he was released. The looks he gave me spoke of regret and apology, but at the same time, of blame and rebuke, perhaps communicating that if I had stayed with him in Boston, we would have realized the dream together, and he wouldn't have gotten mixed up in anything. But while I was with him in Boston, I trusted him completely. He wasn't incapable or unthinking: just the opposite, he was determined to show me the superior side of America as a civilized country, wide enough to encompass all cultures. He invited me to visit Boston's Museum of Science, where I saw one of the first complete dinosaur skeletons in the world and an image of the first x-rays of a man's lung, blackened because of smoking. We went together to the Museum of Fine Arts, and saw paintings by Picasso, Van Gogh, and Frida Kahlo. We plunged deep into thick green forests and saw squirrels, while deer looked at us with a mixture of expectation and affection. He let me wander the Harvard campus and visit MIT. So what happened? Why did it all come crashing down? Did the American dream become the nightmare weighing down on all of our hearts?

His mother called me and my brother. "Rescue Basim," she said, "He's been in Suffolk County Jail in Boston for almost a year, and he's being transferred to another prison." I had come back from Vermont a little earlier. Whenever I missed him, I called him using AT&T's collect telephone service. He was the one who paid for the call. He used to ask me about my family and friends, and about my studies, but suddenly I lost contact with him, and he no longer answered his phone. Someone else was living in the apartment, and didn't provide any details about why Basim wasn't there. After some hesitation, Basim's mother told us that he would have to pay $10,000 in back alimony in order to leave prison. She had been keeping quiet about this news for a long time, until she could pull together the money, and so as not to disgrace herself and her husband in the eyes of the family because her son was in prison in America for scandalous reasons.

She was always timid and kept her own company: she didn't like social interactions and slanderous gossip. She read a lot about religion and became well versed in Islamic law. She always taped the discussions of Shaykh Sha'rawi, which were shown on television every Friday, as well as Arabic music concerts. She was the one who explained to me the meanings of the poem "The Prophet's Hamza" by Ahmad Shawqi, which Umm Kulthum put to music, as well as the meaning of the Sura of Mary in the Qur'an. She told me that the one who fears God will be rewarded beyond reckoning, as it was with Our Lady Mary when she was in the Holy of Holies. She made me love piety and heaven. Perhaps she asked herself how Basim had slipped out of her hands after she had such a tight grip on him as a child: she used to be afraid for him when he fell; when his fledgling wings weren't strong enough, she used to go back and forth with him to school, holding his hand, since he was a student at the same school where she taught music. She hadn't let him run free with his schoolmates or even with his cousins, so he wouldn't act like them. We remember how many times he stood beside her in the middle of a family wedding to sing for us, while she played the song "The Fortune-Teller." How skillful he was in his renditions of most songs and old ballads, to the point that I grew jealous of him. Sometimes I would wonder why my mother wasn't like her—playing pieces by Mozart and Chopin, and filling the empty space of existence with heavenly melodies—instead of always ordering me to study and do my chores. When she was happy, she would sing "First Time in Love" to my father on the bed. And how did it happen that Basim went to Bahrain with his father on a business trip, and sang at a school concert that his mother organized there, honored by both Sultan Qaboos and the president of France for his beautiful voice and his outstanding performance? Who killed this artist in him? Was it his mother, who maintained that hobbies were one thing but a professional career was something else? Or was it the era we're living in that killed off all that was true and creative, because of the public's lack of refined taste? Or is he himself the reason that he neglected his talents, that his will weakened, and that he became incapable of demonstrating them?

❖

Khalid was furious when he learned of the matter, saying that he felt humiliated that he hadn't been informed about what happened to Basim. That it diminished his worth as a man, as a responsible individual, and as a family member legally entitled to make decisions on the family's behalf, despite his young age: he was a businessman who could become one of the most important perfume exporters in Egypt! But there was no value in these assets if a position couldn't be made for him among his family: manhood carries responsibilities in times of crisis.

Khalid collected most of the required money, and I provided the rest, using the money I was going to use to buy a small Fiat, which would rescue me from the hassles of public transportation. Dr. Tariq, a friend of ours who, like his father, worked as an orthopedic doctor, volunteered to go to Boston to deal with the American authorities, pay the money, and free Basim. After a number of negotiations, Basim returned to Egypt, alone and exhausted.

In the car, Basim refused to sit in the front seat beside his father, and instead sat next to me, refusing to talk. His father said he was happy that he'd returned safe and sound, and the cash that was paid didn't mean anything: the cash was thanks to Khalid and Nadir. He continued, saying that Egypt is the "mother of the world," and his being among us was the important thing. He said all that with a tone of sadness, grief, and regret in his voice. Wasn't he the one who had encouraged Basim to emigrate with Jackie, and paid the price of his ticket for him? And wasn't he indulgent with him about the fact that he didn't finish his studies at Cairo University? Didn't he say that the most advanced universities are in the States, and didn't he act as an intermediary for Basim to get his final exemption from military service, in order to facilitate his travel arrangements? Didn't he agree to the despotic verdict of Basim's mother that he not study music and not bring friends over to his apartment? Didn't he also completely keep his son away from any Islamic or cultural influence that would link him to a group that could identify him as belonging to the Egyptian nation? But despite all that, Basim, after devoting his youth to learning, knowledge and music, ended up making women the focus of his entire life

Through the car window, Ataba Square was lit with pale lights. The fire station had been repainted in a way that bore no relation to the art of restoration. The police department was exceptionally evil-looking. Thousands of young men roamed freely with their merchandise in Ataba Square, with pieces of wood in front of them, on which were various kinds of goods, from men's and women's underwear to children's toys, shoes, artificial flowers, and leather watches. From close up he saw policemen chasing the young men selling their wares, who ran off in speed and panic as if there were a rising flood right behind them. *If every one of these people dreams of emigrating to America,* Basim said to himself, *then they have every right to. Who would be satisfied with humiliation and degradation and few options to maneuver out of them? You're still in love with the people who imprisoned you and humiliated you. Instead of returning to Egypt with a checkbook in my hand, I've come back in handcuffs.*

He looked at the National Theater which appeared like a giant tent whose sides were covered in dust and spiders. He remembered New York with its lit-up streets and noisy theaters, it strip clubs and dance performances, its jazz and blues. As though he were in a long nightmare, the streets of the city he used to walk in passed before him: the tall buildings, the clean streets, and the different means of transportation in all their varieties, as if it were humanity's right to live life to the fullest. Then he asked himself, why don't we build our houses the way they do? It was raining and water was forming puddles in the potholes and bumps on the curbs and in the middle of the streets. He remembered the rain that would pour down like a flood; then, after it stopped, not a single puddle could be seen, since there were drains that swallowed up all the water. *Can't Egyptians benefit from the expertise of others?* he asked himself. *Are we tormenting ourselves by not struggling to change our current circumstances? Or will things remain as they are because we have been turned to stone like the columns at Karnak Temple, or the stone blocks of the pyramids? What has your civilization gained for you but insults and humiliation?* He remembered his situation in

118

prison, and the pain he was subjected to at the hands of the guards and his fellow prisoners. *Civilization has its cost*, he said to himself, *and freedom has its price that must be paid*.

As he was getting out of the car, he handed me a folder that contained a number of sheets of paper. "Hold on to it," he said. "I know you love writing; maybe it will help you write a story one day."

You find in it papers containing the memoirs and diaries Basim wrote on his distant travels that you read and reread, wondering how it would be possible for you to create a story out of them that bears some resemblance to what he wrote. You leave it and go to sleep, only to wake up and find some of these papers scattered over the mattress; the rest you see on the floor, soaked in the water the housekeeper poured out to clean the room with, as your wife asked her to. You get up from sleep in a panic, and gather up the remaining papers, and get into an argument with her as you try to make her understand that what she's done is a crime. She tells you that the greatest crime is filth. You try to read what Basim wrote but the water obliterated them, wiping them clean. You hit upon the idea of drying the remaining pages with the iron, but only a little writing was visible. So you try to complete with your imagination what was lacking in reality.

This is the story Basim told in these tattered pages.

New Hampshire, 1998

The name Basim, meaning 'smiling' in Arabic, puts an ironic smile on my face: since I entered this prison, I haven't laughed once. I didn't smile once the entire month I spent alone in-prison, without a friend or another voice I could hear in my solitary cell, except some graffiti that wasn't in my English–Arabic dictionary. I was arrested with no warning while I was entering the building where I lived in Brighton. I was held for a long time for some reason. There were several charges against me: the first was assault and battery against my wife to get her to admit that what was growing inside her was my son. I wanted a child, not only so I could get permanent residency status, but also to feel that I really existed. Even though with children there would be someone to carry on my name, sometimes I really hated the idea of them—they're a heavy burden, and it's so beautiful for a person to live without the feeling of responsibility for the future, for children. You just live or die with no problems to worry about.

The biggest charge against me concerned the fines the court had imposed on me because of the divorce, which I couldn't pay off, so I was sent to prison. Finally, there was the charge of providing cover for aiding and abetting a female spy working for the Russian intelligence services, whom I realized was Olga. I became certain of it after I discovered that my father's secret documents that I had brought with me from Cairo had been stolen. I thought I would sell them in the U.S., or perhaps they would help me write a political book like the ones by Muhammad Hasanein Heikal, which I had read in Cairo. He was a personal friend of my father, and I heard a lot about the Camp David Accords from him, despite my being so young.

Heikal was strongly opposed to Sadat, and stirred up public opinion against him. For his part, Sadat hated Heikal, and wanted to get rid of him by any means possible. Sadat had a number of secret dossiers about the Camp David proceedings, which my father would draw up to hand over to him. They would often be rejected, because Sadat didn't agree with his father's position, and so, for a lot of things, Sadat would work out the plans himself. Osama al-Baz and Ahmad Maher were closer to Sadat than my father was, and their advice met his approval. My father felt frustrated by Carter as a participant in the peace process and his control over the situation during the negotiations between Egypt and Israel, especially pertaining to Israel's withdrawal to the 1948 borders, and implementing UN Resolution 242, which gave the Palestinians the right to self-determination and self-government, not only the administration of internal affairs.

I took my father's documents that pertained to Jerusalem: its status in the treaty, since the Palestinians had agreed to negotiations and the signing of the treaty, and about how whoever controls the city should be trustworthy, and whether Jerusalem would become the Israeli capital, an Arab capital, or a neutral zone. My father was entirely responsible for it on the orders of Sadat himself. He also had transcriptions of audiotapes of conversations held between Menachem Begin, Carter, and Sadat. I took them all with me after making photocopies of them.

There were also letters exchanged between them, corresponding at great length about this subject, and even Sadat's decision to arrest the Communists and the Muslim Brothers who opposed the drawing up of the treaty. In my father's desk was the list with their names, which I stole from his office. Or perhaps my father went easy on that order after he found himself out of the loop following Sadat's assassination, when Mubarak took over the government.

I had been addicted to Olga, and I was an expert in making her happy; even after she made up with George, she would come to my place and stay all night long with me. She began to circulate inside me like my own blood, and became my pulse. I let her get her hands on my things and on my body. She knew the outlines of my arteries and the number of pores on my skin, and she could count the beauty marks found on different parts of me, even in sensitive places. Likewise, I knew her pleasure zones and the secret places of her arousal. I would always relieve her of her exhaustion after she returned from fashion shows by massaging her body with mineral oil and Libyan olive oil. For her part, she would light the candles she loved so much and set them in places scattered throughout the apartment, creating an atmosphere of tranquility, silence, and simplicity. She also meddled with my papers, notebooks, and music albums. We became lovers whose nights were illuminated by candles and surrounded by music; nights that well up with the pleasure of trysts and of satiating our thirsts, as if we were in a moment of gentle Sufi luminosity, even when she went back to George for no reason, while claiming that he wasn't easy to deal with, and that he might slit her throat one night with a knife in a dark corner as she comes out of the theater: no one would rescue her or take an interest in her, especially since she didn't have the legal documents to remain in America. So it was better to go along with him. She convinced me that he was impotent, and that the only thing he needed was some cash and for her to acknowledge that he was doing her a favor.

I woke up and found a letter in which she confessed her love for me, but said that her love for George was stronger and greater because he was from her country, and in this lonely country she couldn't find protection with foreigners like myself who have nothing going for them except a warm kiss and pleasure—I wasn't the only one capable of unleashing that

122

pleasure in her, and this world is full of men. Before she finished her letter by signing "Insincerely Yours," she said "Thank Nadir for me: he made me feel human without asking anything in return, even if we didn't eat the forbidden fruit together, the way I did with you."

Concerning the secret documents, she said it was inevitable that she would steal them: it was her mission, which she had been assigned by the Russian spy services—she was very loyal to her nation's causes. The Soviet Union had suffered so much from its disintegration, caused by American meddling in its affairs, but she was certain that Russians should be ruling the world too. They wouldn't let the world be ruled by a group of people who have no heritage and no literature. We are the ones, she said, who taught the world how to dance ballet; the writings of Tolstoy, Chekhov, and Dostoevsky are the source of modern wisdom. The documents were very important, she added, because they would help Russia learn Israel and America's secret plans for the Middle East, and then it would be possible for Russia to share in understanding the master plan for the future, not only for the Middle East, but for the world. On the whole, she added, this was for the benefit of Egypt and the Arabs. She said that she promised to return them if the documents proved to have no real value: she isn't as despicable as someone in her position should be, but she has assignments she has to carry out, and pleasure is more appealing when there's some profit in it.

Winter

Prison wasn't as bad as I had thought, especially after another prisoner shared the same room with me. He was African-American, with a good-looking face and dark skin. He looked just like the actor Sidney Poitier. He claimed he had been imprisoned for his attacks on Christianity. This was something strange coming from a country that permitted freedom of religious beliefs. He said that a sentence of prison or burning at the stake was issued against him by the Vatican, as used to be done for witches and sorcerers in a not-too-distant era, since they were said to be agents of demons on earth. This prisoner, who was called Mado, said that the Messiah has black skin and African features. He said the Messiah has African origins and that his family immigrated to Palestine, in flight from enslavement. He said that the Messiah isn't from the white race at all. Mado had started going to all the museums and hurling black tar at paintings of Jesus and the Virgin Mary in order to disfigure them. Each time, he was able to get away, despite the many security cameras keeping watch over the galleries. Then he was arrested several times while preaching to people in Harvard Square, urging them to believe in the "Black Messiah," who came to liberate the slaves of Africa and America from the arrogant power of whites, their oppression, and their tyranny, and that he would come again to free the blacks and kill the Antichrist. He called on people to destroy all the images of a white Jesus, and not feel compassion for His mother or her sad eyes at the crucifixion scene, because that man is not the Messiah. Mado ordered his friends and black disciples to spread this gospel everywhere in Boston by collecting donations that would be spent on this missionary activity. He was arrested while in possession of a counterfeit ten-dollar bill that a white man had given him. He claimed he had been charged with putting into circulation counterfeit money with God's name on it, and with slandering Jesus and Christianity.

He would only sleep completely naked. He masturbated every night, and taught me to do that, too. He made me not feel guilty about it.

On his body, which bore an African strength and solidity, there was a tattoo of a cross running the length of his body, starting from the top of his collarbone, with the cross-piece running along his arms, and then splitting above his crotch before descending down his thighs.

❖

Screams in the prison's recesses coming from . . . . Filthy water dripping down all sides of the cell.

Plastic bags . . . naked bodies mounting each other . . . electric cords and shocks and trembling bodies . . . human odors—perhaps coming from isolated areas—from the bodies of convicts.

Insults: *Son of a bitch, A-rab, n****r.*

My suicide attempt using one of the plastic bags, by putting it over my head and face, to be rid of this life. . . .

❖

The game of chess—which I tried to teach Nadir, and which he failed at, because of his intense love of reading and his complete antipathy to strategy and planning, possessions and defended positions—a game I learned from my friends at school, where I got advanced rankings, and even won the national championship. I beat the cleverest chess players among the American expats at the Maadi Club. It became my only pastime in prison: my chess skills left the prisoners and guards speechless. They placed sizable bets on my winning this game, to the point that my matches were broadcast on the air on World Human Rights Day, so that the state could prove it was being

125

lenient even with prisoners and foreigners. Eventually, Mado told me, "Why are you letting them use you like that? They're not bragging about you: they're bragging about themselves and their arrogance, so people will say that whites are the greatest race in existence. Forget about this game—try finding yourself another hobby."

❖

I was very weak during those days: I didn't get enough food, and the weather was very cold. The snow, which I could see through my iron-barred window, never stopped falling. There were no birds in the sky. Sometimes I would imagine winged angels coming to me, their wings retracting in order to pass between the iron bars. They would smile at me, and touch my hair with their wings or their fingers as Olga claimed when she told Nadir her story.

I imagined they were the spirit of my mother calling on me in her prayers to return safely to her. I didn't dare write to her and tell her about what happened, I was afraid she would be despondent or have something terrible happen to her: my mother, with soft hair flowing down over her back and over her forehead like an Arabian mare, purebred like the Eastern fillies famous for their splendor, beauty, and nobility. And that well-proportioned body of hers, and her long, slender legs that used to mesmerize me even when she revealed them in front of my father. What would I say to her—that I've been a failure in my life abroad, and that I'm a convict? That would be too much for her. She was the golden child in her family, which was made up entirely of women. All of her sisters were able to give their children the best education—some of them became doctors and engineers. She was the one who protected me from anything that was harmful, to the point that she would lock the doors when she went out, in view of my fascination with the world outside my house since childhood. When I learned to crawl, she would tie up one of my feet so I couldn't get into the bathroom and fall into the bath or otherwise hurt myself. Now the family will be talking about nothing but her failure. In the end, I wrote to her when I got sick with a cough that didn't get better. I was very depressed and remained in a dangerous state. A prison cell is no good for ordinary people, so imagine what it's like for a frail person like me.

❖

Mado asked me about my religion one day, so I told him I was Muslim, although not a practicing one, but that nevertheless I believed that this world has a Creator, and that life wasn't created by accident, they way materialists and atheists believed. When I immigrated to the United States, the first thing I put in my suitcase was a prayer rug and the Holy Qur'an. It wasn't just my idea, but my mother's, too: she told me that the Qur'an would keep me safe. Then she recited, as she passed her hands over my head, *"He who has given you the Qur'an will surely bring you back to the place of return,"* that is, to Mecca. It was a verse that can be widely interpreted, so I will definitely get back to Cairo, because the Word of God is truthful, and praying will keep me away from wickedness and sin. Despite the sins I've committed, I'm a believer. I love all the prophets, and I believe in their message. It doesn't interest me whether the Messiah was white or black, I glorify and cherish him, since he was devoted to his mother. He wasn't a wicked oppressor. I said all that, although Mado was angry with me because I failed to reassure him that I believed in his preaching about the skin color of the Messiah. However, he continued to listen to me, and wanted to learn more about Islam. He was extremely eager to find out about the skin color of our Prophet Muhammad, as well as the foundational principles of his mission, especially about his belief that all humans are equal, regardless of skin color.

Mado told me that he could pray so that the sun would reach us, or that he could read aloud verses from the Bible in my ear, and I would be healed from my cough, just like the Messiah had done. But in Boston, there was no sun in this season of winter, and his prayers and seclusion met with no success.

"Warmth and milk are the cure, and also getting out of this prison." That's what the doctor whose job it was to treat me said. He was a Palestinian living in the United States, who dreamed of returning to Palestine to treat those injured in the intifada, but he was married to an American woman who told him, "If you go there, you can forget about your wife and children—consider us dead." So he asked to be transferred from the large hospital he was working in. He preferred to treat unfortunate patients, especially foreigners and Arabs; he assured me that healing comes from God.

He told me that I reminded him of his son, who he once dreamed of living with in Jerusalem, and praying with him there. They were going to buy a small house there and grow lemon and olive trees in front of it. But his wife and her stubbornness killed every hope he had of getting his wish. It was too much for him now to fight over it and begin again. He assured me that any hope for my recovery lies in my willpower, and that the cause of my sickness is frustration and despair that I would never get out. He advised me to write to my mother and family in Egypt, "The people of Egypt are all gallantry and vigor. They are the backbone of the Arab nation." That's what he said, as he laughed and spoke in Egyptian dialect, as if he were Gamal Abd al-Nasser.

I was afraid I would die and no one would know about it. My feelings of loneliness, fear, and guilt swelled up, and the moment I picked up the pen I hesitated to tell my mother the whole story of my situation. My mother was the daughter of a simple man whose grandfather had worked as a sergeant major in the Egyptian army and had joined Ahmad Urabi's uprising. He said he had marched from the city of Zagazig to Cairo to stand with Urabi in opposition to the khedive, to criticize injustice and tyranny. He had also fought in the battle of Tell al-Kabir, in which Urabi was defeated as a result of a betrayal. Her father inherited a love of knowledge and was blessed with seven daughters. He felt no disgrace about that, and didn't scowl once at his wife over it, but he was determined to give his daughters an excellent upbringing, and he raised them to be decent and modest. Each one of them got a good education, and they all married husbands who had high standing in society. My father saw her when he was on an assignment in Zagazig, as she was coming out of the teachers' college carrying a violin. She was like the noonday sun walking delicately on the ground. He fell in love with her and followed her as far as her house. He didn't leave until he had set the wedding date.

She came to Cairo, alone in a world she didn't know much about, except for some stories she had read or plots from radio series, which she used to follow along with on the "Voice of the Arabs" station, at five o'clock along with her mother and her young sisters. She was afraid of this open world, and so shut herself off from it, like the country bumpkin shocked by the city's unfriendliness and its enormous size. My father, on the other hand, wouldn't allow her to go out except on special occasions to visit relatives. But she was working hard at her music, and wanted to prove to the Cairo women that she was better than them, that art recognizes no boundaries, and that talent and commitment are the basis for a young woman's success.

She used to be a big fan of the singer Nagat al-Saghira. She was impressed by her elegance, and used to sing her songs, especially the one she sang with the lyrics by Nizar Qabbani:

> Love for the land is part of our imagination
> If we don't find it there, then we'll invent it.

She had Nagat al-Saghira's affectionate glances, and her romantic heartbeat. Her laugh would ring out more sweetly than the music of the violin she played. In her family, she was a living symbol of elegance and artistry.

My emotional daydreaming was cut short by an intense pain in my chest, and I heard the voice of the guard yelling at some other prisoners, so I hurried to write to her. I told her about the whole affair. She sent me a letter and set my mind at ease. She said that she still loved me and would respect me for as long as I lived, and she would work hard to get me out of this prison. She urged me to read the Sura of Joseph, and to ask God to free me from captivity, because He provides deliverance for His pious servants. I laughed and cried, wondering, *am I one of these pious servants?* I did nothing but wicked things, but to tell the truth, every woman I made love to was my wife: before being intimate with her, I acknowledged her as my wife, and made clear that what we were doing had nothing to do with illicit sex. I would insist on writing a temporary marriage contract, by which I would acknowledge

130

before God that I was married to her, and that she accepted me as her husband. Don't believe for a minute that I am a cheat, but I am a man you could call lustful. God placed in me a love for women, the same way that Nadir loves books, learning, traveling, and talking with people. All of us have our immoderate desires.

Spring

With the coming of spring, God brought me back to health, and the sun that Mado had prayed for so much to rise over our cell shone strongly. I recovered and began to do exercises. I avoided talking to the addicts and perverts, but didn't try to provoke them. I only revealed the melancholy side of my personality, so they thought that I was mentally ill and avoided me completely. I was helped in that by my western features, which gave the impression that I was an American, not a desperate immigrant.

❖

Dr. Tariq was a fair-haired young man who was on the short side. He spoke fluent English, if you paid no attention to some stammering and unexplained pauses, and he had an excellent character. He met me, smiled, and assured me that I was innocent —thanks to his conversation with the lawyer who he had entrusted with my defense in order to get me released once the money had been paid. "There is injustice everywhere," he said. "But in a foreign country, don't give them the opportunity to treat you arrogantly. Most of them are cruel-hearted, but with the law and money on your side, you will get your rights. So don't be afraid."

"Khalid and Nadir are like my brothers," he added, "and you are now like my brother Tamir who lives in Canada." Tariq met with the official in charge of my release, and explained my circumstances to him. But he didn't take any interest in my case, so Tariq paid the debt, and here I've been waiting to get out since then, alone in a cell after Mado left, when it was decided that he shouldn't be in prison, but in a mental hospital. Before Mado left, he drew a big cross on the wall, and beside it a rising sun, and a mouth with a big smile, with my name written on it. The mouth looked a lot like mine.

❖

Handing over possessions . . . an intense feeling of weakness. A cassette tape, a notebook of personal diaries, sleeping pills, cough medicine, a change of clothes, policemen . . . airplane, a horrible droning noise, an airplane like it was about to fall into the ocean; night and day. Very weak vision . . . intense heat—lots of crowds.

The above is what I tried to write and add to from Basim's diaries, most of which were blotted out.

Cairo, 2000

These days you will see Basim downtown, sitting at the al-Bustan Coffeeshop, or holding hands with a girl, maybe Japanese or American, or a tourist from somewhere. You can also see him in a perfume store, or in a tourist shop that sells papyrus. He looks the seller in the eye to make him understand that he has a female client with him who is looking to buy, and so he should jack up the price of his wares so that Basim can get his cut of it. You'll see him wearing clothes that look like what foreigners are wearing, their formal outfits and casual styles. You'll see his face, radiant like the faces of foreigners. He walks like they do, too—with energy, overconfidence, and wonder. He smiles with confidence and experience.

At the end of the night, he will go to one of the dark, narrow side streets in the Kom al-Samn district to buy heroin. It's to help him relax, and to sleep deeply. He will dim the light in his room as much as possible. That way it won't remind him of the neon light the Americans used to inflict on him as a kind of torture, until he confessed to beating his wife. He will open all the windows in the biting cold of winter, in order to see the stars. In the daytime, he will intentionally look at the sun he was deprived of seeing in prison. He recalls Mado and how he preached to him of salvation. A year after he comes back from America, he will come to rely on a Jewish Canadian girl named Judy, whom he came to know in Sharm al-Sheikh after she had visited Israel. After they had met several times, she claimed that she was his blood relation, since Arabs and Jews come from one race and are cousins. She declared that the reason she clung to him was that she saw in a vision that the Adam's rib from which she was created was the same as the one that belonged to an Egyptian; that he had come to America to look for her, but failed to find her there because she wasn't American. And so she came to him to complete his missing part, and to search for the meaning of the east between the legs of an Egyptian man whose semen might grant her the essence of eternal life.

She is the daughter of a wealthy Canadian who owned a number of businesses. Basim invites her to live with him and she welcomes the idea; although the apartment is hardly suitable for living in, she will say it's not important. She will buy some indoor plants to give him a feeling of living in a natural forest, and she will hang on the walls a picture of a beautiful girl carrying a child in her arms, or a piece of carpet she bought from an old man in the Tentmaker's district, which will breathe life into the apartment. In one corner, you will see some English-language novels by Stephen King or John Grisham, or a novel with an old jacket by Charles Dickens, *David Copperfield*, or Jane Austen's *Pride and Prejudice*. And from the current era, you will find a single Arabic novel, Alaa Al Aswany's *The Yacoubian Building*.

You will find a small cat which will grow to full size over the course of the few times you visit him. He will tell you that he bought it at the Friday Souq in the Sayyida Aisha neighborhood, and that Judy took pity on it, being so thin and emaciated, and that she treated it, especially in its sensitive spots, and fed it until it grew bigger. She is afraid for its safety from the male cats that lie in wait for it on the staircase. Basim will tell you that he knows for certain it isn't a purebred Siamese cat, but is a mixed breed. He doesn't keep the cat from coming in and out, although he had made a square-shaped iron door for her. The door had another benefit for him, as protection for his empty apartment against thieves. When Judy commented that it looked like a prison door, he said, "Life is one big prison."

She will pay the rent for the apartment, which has no furniture other than an old sofa that his mother had let him borrow, and a filthy mattress covered with semen, bloodstains, and sweat from long nights when foreign girls who came for different reasons slept on it. The apartment is lit by fifty-watt bulbs. She will buy him a Volkswagen, and she will pay his electricity and water bills, and pay the rent for him for the previous year and the next. She will go with him to meet tourists and share in his profits, but woe unto him if he should have sex with another woman. She will think about having a baby one day, but she is afraid of giving birth to twins because her mother gave birth to fraternal twins, of which she is one. She will be very happy about being friends with Nadir. She will say that he is romantic, and that girls will cheat on him a lot because he is so nice and easygoing. She will say he is a genius and he will make a great writer because of his sensitivity. She will go with Basim after Nadir pulls some strings for them so they can work in the Auberge Hotel in Fayoum: Basim in reception, and Judy as head of cleaning services. Nadir will also serve as a witness to their urfi marriage, after the hotel's manager said it would be necessary to smooth the way for them to reside and work in the hotel, and so that the Jews and Arabs could reconcile with each other with this marriage. They will live in a room reserved for them alone, with a comfortable bed, and a big mirror that Judy will sit in front of as she rubs her delicate skin with Nivea cream to protect it from the sun's burning rays. It also has a bath with gushing water, warmed by the action of a solar-cell heater located above the top of the room. Basim will linger for long nights beside the enchanted Lake Qarun, and he will tell her a lot about Qarun whose castle God caused to be swallowed up by the earth. But she loves the place because her Jewish forebears lived there, and she wears the veil so the local farmers won't harass her when they ride the microbus from Fayoum to Cairo. She will go to visit his mother, who is very fond of her, because she is innocent and young and stands beside Basim, helping him to re-acclimatize to living in Egypt. She will enter all the homes of Basim's extended family, and get to know all its members, and she will ask a lot of detailed questions. Basim will be pleased by her zealous love of knowing and learning.

Basim's mother will tell all the family members that Judy is kind and polite and will point out especially that she is a vegetarian, and when it comes to fish, she prefers to eat only cuttlefish. Judy's mother will come to Cairo to take her with her and rescue her from Basim after she learned all about what happened to him in Boston and in prison. And isn't America's judgment the final word, the automatic calculator that preserves all data about everyone in existence, especially if they are Muslims and Arabs? She will come to Nadir's house, where he will give her a wonderful welcome, and will show off his best behavior. He will prepare for her and for Judy a table of food, since it was a holiday. Judy's mother seemed happy to be there in Maadi, and said that it was a lot like the neighborhood where she lived in Canada. She looked Middle Eastern, which made Nadir suspect that she was an Israeli Arab, but she said that she was a Bulgarian who had immigrated to Canada a long time ago with her mother, fleeing Nazi persecution of the Jews. She said she found Canada a suitable place to live, but she always dreamed of a nation that she would return to one day. Then she mentioned that she began life as a worker in a small diamond-cutting and jewelry-making workshop, and that she became forewoman in a few months, and came close to running her own business in that field, if the owner of the store hadn't asked her one day to travel to South Africa. She believed it was for a training period or to visit mining sites, but once she was there, he asked her to hide some stones in one of her cosmetic cases, and in some sensitive areas on her body. She refused, she said, because by that point, she had fallen in love with a South African man, Judy's father, and she was pregnant with Judy. She didn't want to sacrifice her love for the sake of money. She agreed to live with Judy's father, despite his poverty, and with some small diamond stones that a black worker had given her, she helped him escape with a forged work contract that would allow him to work in Belgium, where another branch of the factory was located. She laughed, and said that she almost fell in love with him only because of the beauty and fullness of his lips. With these uncut stones, she and Judy's father were able to buy their own business, then sell it at a profit. Then they founded an agency for buying businesses, and in the course of a few years, it became a large economic powerhouse in the city they were living in. She said, "Don't think anyone in the world helped us! We helped each other, once we understood the conspiracy that has been going on against us ever since the Nazi era." Then she said, "We Jews are like pandas: we have to be protected. We are threatened with extinction from hunters and predators on all sides. The only thing the hunter cares about is whether there is any profit to be made from our hides and pelts. Even if we are rescued, we are destined for zoos where we can be safe, and at the same time, living proof that our species still exists these days." Nadir responds to her by saying, "And the children of Palestine die in their refugee camps, and when the Zionists fire at them, their corpses rot for lack of refrigerators to keep their precious bodies preserved for burial." She answered, "Against a terrorist nation, anything is permissible . . ."

". . . if you don't have a conscience," Nadir said, finishing her sentence. She got angry: "Your tolerance for the right of the Jews to have their own nation is doubtful," she said, "while the Palestinians can make a nation for themselves with few concessions and little tolerance." Nadir laughed and then was silent, because he didn't want to ruin the gathering with heavy talk about politics. Basim kept out of it and stayed quiet, listening to the argument, tying to connect its parts to distill some wisdom from it. Perhaps he believed that she would give her blessing to this relationship with her daughter, believing that she struggled with her husband from the beginning, and pretending to be completely unaware of the concept of Jews. . . .

❖

After Judy and her mother leave your apartment, Basim will call you that night to tell you that Judy's mother snatched her away without telling him and that he was going to kill himself. So you go to him and find him having a breakdown, clutching a razor blade so he can cut his wrists. You calm him down, and wipe away his tears. You try to make him get up off the carpet and you listen to his stories from the beginning. He tells you she was the only one who gave his life meaning, that she was affectionate and kind, and that life has been empty of all meaning since the moment she left. In every corner of this place she left behind a beautiful memory and a spirit of creativity, and a scent of perfume. For the first time, you know the meaning of love, and you feel the emotions of lovers. You feel grief, and feel jealous toward him. You hope this feeling continues to dwell within you, even if it costs you your life. You tell him the separation was expected, even inevitable, and that she was like other women who had to leave his life and eventually travel back to their country. That her mother didn't come to bless her daughter's marriage to him, but to rescue her from him, and that Judy went along with her mother's plan. That's why she traveled without saying goodbye, even though one time he noticed a plane ticket in Judy's name, which her mother had left lying on the table. But he didn't approach Judy about it. He assumed there was a ticket for him in another bag, that it was waiting there as a surprise for him. But the surprise was Judy's departure, which made him feel like she'd been kidnapped from him in broad daylight, in front of people, by a group of young thugs, and there was nothing he could do about it, as if he were drugged.

❖

A Conspiracy

Like the fates that conspire against certain people and steal happiness from them, the conspiracy by Judy and her mother against you was definite and final. That's what you tell Basim, in order to make it easier on him, but he rejects that, explaining to himself that Judy is innocent and pure, so it would be difficult for her to betray him. Then he drags himself weakly over the carpet, and hands you a letter that Judy sent him before she departed. In it, she said he was a mirage like the sands that shimmer from a distance: the thirsty person reckons it to be water, but it is deceptive. She said she was thirsty for his love, and that she quenched her thirst in it until his water flowed over her, and nearly drowned her. That she had to pull her head out from the depths of his ocean-like love, so that she could live and breathe, rather than drown and dissolve in it. Then she added,

> *"My mother didn't force me to leave, but she helped me do it. I had to avoid your gravitational pull so that I could free myself from your orbit. Don't think that I deceived you, or that your happiness has come to an end, but I had to disappear, so that you could know if you were happy with me or not. I gave you all I had, and here I am trying out your gift. Yes, all your kindnesses were more than enough, but your work*

140

*and the efforts you were making were imperfect and
incomplete. Yes, you didn't ask me for too much
money, but materially I felt that I represented
something important for you. I had to leave so that
you can rely on yourself, and know the meaning of
hard work. I've made a lot of sacrifices—you know
that. I've given up my religion for your sake: do
you know that I am considered an 'apostate' in the
teachings of the Talmud? And that by marrying a
Muslim, I've lost my religious identity? Even though
you didn't compel me to convert to Islam, and not
once did you hint that you wanted me to embrace it!
You reprimanded Nadir once for trying to talk to me
with enthusiasm about your religion and its worth.
You've given me so much: I am indebted to you, the
strength of your sincerity, and your commitment to
me all this time. But my family believes you're different
from me, and thinks I am still too young to take on
the responsibility of marriage. My trip to Israel and
then Egypt was an experience I had to undertake, so
I could test my ability to live with someone else on my
own, and try to discover the world. But my guiding
star pointed me to your position. I said, 'I will be with
you where you are, because you were the only Arab
who treated me as a lover, a friend, and a fellow
human being, not a pig or a monkey to be avoided or
rejected.' Instead, you wished me well and opened your
arms and heart to me. You killed the myth of hatred
between Jews and Arabs. You cut short thousands of
years of hatred and bad blood, and I came to you with
all my love, I drank your pouring rain, and I bathed*

in your fragrant perfume. You became my nation, my
family, and my world, but I still have a lot ahead of
me to learn, not just the language of love and the body.
There is my mind, which needs to be developed, and
art that I should be studying and making. I want to
finish college, which I left before graduating, and
finish the books that have been collecting dust since I
came to Cairo. I don't deny that you've awoken my
senses and made me a new woman. I see the world
with the eyes of a woman in love, but where am I now?
I should be moving to another stage: my body has had
its fill. Now it's the spirit's turn to be filled. I had no
choice but to leave."

He hugged the letter to his chest, then turned to face the wall and burst into tears. You leave him to be by himself, and emerge from the building into the pitch-black darkness.

He will come to your house numerous times to use the computer to write e-mails to Judy. He will sit there for hours, without getting tired. You will become annoyed by his presence sometimes, and feel that there is no use in what he's doing, telling him, "She's gone and she's not coming back."

Then he comes to you and tells you, "Nadir, I printed out all the e-mails that Judy and I have sent each other for you. I believe she will get back together with me, because it is the most beautiful love story in the world. She is the brightest, most tender woman I've ever met in my life, and of all of them, she knows the most about me and my situation.

"Really?" you respond. "Did you really know them all? Or are they strangers like you, and the only things you have in common are natural impulses and a desire to explore more bodies?" Love is something completely separate from what goes on in your bed."

He will tell you that he's waived his author's rights for this love story: he will be satisfied if you give him the first copy signed: *To Judy and Basim forever*.

Later, he'll tell you that he wants to travel to see her but can't, because he lost his passport and has problems with the national military draft, and several big ongoing court cases in a country still ruled by emergency laws and an official police record. He didn't finish his education in America, and can't find temporary work. He can't get access to the cash he deposited in one of the banks there, because the federal government seized it, perhaps out of a suspicion that this cash belonged to Olga, who was spying on the United States for the benefit of the Russian intelligence services, but he will sue the federal government by means of a global legal association that specializes in human rights, which has a substantial web presence. He had begun corresponding with them and there was some hope that he would get his money back. Another time, he meets you as you are coming out of the Cairo Atelier. He greets you warmly, but doesn't take an interest in you or your wife—who doesn't understand you and from whom you want to separate—or your problems in the university, or your impossible attempts to write a text that is genuine, that will live on after your death. He offers to give you a lift, anywhere you want, and then invites you to his house in the remote neighborhood called "The Foundry" in Nasr City. You hesitate to go with him, because it's late and you have a lot of things to do, but he lures you by saying it's a chance for you both to hear some music: he will perform for you a piece by Omar Khorshid that Khorshid had played at an Abd al-Halim Hafez concert. He reminds you that Khorshid was killed in an accident on Pyramids Road, perhaps because of an illicit relationship with the daughter of one of the country's powerful men. You refuse to go, so he asks to borrow some money from you. You don't hesitate to give it to him because you're Nadir—generous, a pushover, the same Nadir who remembers how he gave you a royal welcome in venerable Harvard Square, and how he hosted you in his house, and how he used to give you cash to go to the movies, perhaps so he could be alone with Olga for a little while, and how he stole a t-shirt to give to you as a gift. How he let you share his bed with him—he didn't approve of you sleeping on the floor like a dog. And how he pleaded with you to stay with him. Nor will you forget the trip where he took you with him to the Atlantic Ocean, something you had dreamed about for so long, and you swam in it and you ended up telling your family that you were dazzled by America, assuring them that Basim was there and successful and was living the dream. When you loan him money, you feel sorry for his situation, and wish that you could bring him with you to your house to give him a hot dinner, and make him feel he's still alive, but your wife, who goes to sleep early, is afraid and refuses to have strangers as guests, but you don't pay any attention to her, and do what you like with him.

❖

The days will pass, while Basim remains as he is. Judy has gone, and other women will take her place. Egyptian women and others from his stable of women will enter the scene.

Nadia comes into Basim's life as a girl who helps him snag foreigners. Basim will marry her in an urfi ceremony when she is sixteen. On several occasions, he will meet her downtown in front of the Dar al-Shorouk Bookstore. She will always wear beige jeans and a shirt of the same color, with a short jacket over it. You will take pity on her when you see her, and feel bad about the situation she's in when she says that she should be at her house now, studying her lessons, or cleaning the house with her sisters, or talking on the phone with a boy she knows, making her family believe it's a girlfriend of hers from school. He will introduce her to you, and she will talk with ease, with an innocence in her eyes that makes you cry for her. You hope you can help her get out of this whole business.

Another time you will meet her, when you're wandering by yourself, and you will invite her to have tea with you at Café Riche. The owner of the restaurant will be amazed to find you with her: he knows you very well, and those sitting with him will look at her with disapproval, but it doesn't matter. You invite her to dinner, and during the conversation, she confesses that she loves Basim, even though he forces her to do things she doesn't like, like buying drugs for him so he can keep his girlfriends happy. When you leave the place, you will meet Basim and tell him what she said. He will tell you about how she is both good and bad at the same time, because she claimed he was the father of the baby she was carrying. He had no idea whose it was, and even if it was his, why hadn't she told him about it before? He will ask you to lend him the money for an abortion, but you refuse to. You tell him he should be marrying her officially instead of treating her badly like this.

You long to know what happened to Nadia, and later you will learn that she had an abortion, that she wears the veil now, that she went back to school, and that she still loves Basim despite his betrayal of her. But you tell her she was wrong to get herself into that predicament. You treat her as though she were one of your students or a cousin of yours, just as you did with Olga. You walk with her downtown and invite her to have some sweets from Groppi with you. You buy her flowers and she says it's the first time anyone has bought her red roses. She reminds you that today is Valentine's Day, and you laugh at the coincidence. You will see tears and sadness in Nadia's eyes, and you wish you could do something to cheer her up, but when she spots a foreign woman, she leaves you. You disapprove of this behavior, but she apologizes, saying, "Let me do it. I'm going to go and try make some money. I'm poor and defenseless. I'm not like Basim: his father is rich and in the intelligence service. My father is a worker in a glass factory in Shubra al-Khayma, and my mother doesn't lead a life of leisure either." She thanks you and is amazed that you and Basim are related. She gives you her address and asks you to write to her, but you don't do it because you lose it. She tells you that she always sits in the After Eight Coffeeshop or at the Mashrabiya or the Trellis, where you can eat fuul or sip tea. And that she sometimes stands in front of Felfela Restaurant where foreigners gather so she can strike up a conversation with them, or have some kushari, or shawerma. You always pass by these places: perhaps you will see her and tell her she should be studying, that she should go back to school, and that you can help her.

Nadia will tell you how her father lost his job after the factory he was working in became privatized, that his fixed pension was not enough to feed five children, that her mother can barely scrape together their daily food, and that her father is completely out of work because he is frail and incapable of strenuous physical activity, and you believe her because she too has a slight frame and is skinny, like a small girl who hasn't fully grown. She confesses to you that none of the neighbors or the family knows except her father who is grateful to her for shouldering the responsibility along with him. He knows that having one daughter go to ruin isn't like having the whole family going to ruin. He met Basim several times and begged him to do the right thing and marry her, asking him to use his influence with his father to find a job for him. She will tell you how she was afraid of this father of his, that it was Basim's father who ruined her life and his son's life through his cruelty and lack of concern for him, ever since the day Basim was born. She will say that one time she and Basim saw him sitting with a girl a lot younger than he at the Abu Shaqra Restaurant in Qasr al-Aini, and that he wasn't embarrassed to see them, and didn't invite them even to drink or eat, although for two days the two of them hadn't eaten anything but peanuts. This man does things that he forbids his son from doing. She will tell you that he's no saint, and doesn't act his age. On several occasions, he had tried to seduce her, against her will, when she and Basim were visiting him. She could have told Basim, but she didn't want to add to the hostility and resentment between the two of them. But one day, she'll explode at him, and tell him that he is a terrible person, and that he doesn't deserve to be called a father or even a human being, that she may be small in size and young, but she does have a big heart, and that she is capable of shouldering responsibility and sticking with Basim to the end, because she really and truly loves him. She will say that he is everything to her, and he has made up for all the deprivation she had known in her life; that she doesn't love him because he comes from a good family, or a powerful one, but because he is affectionate, and knows how to treat women, and he's a man in the full sense of the word. She will say how faithful she is to Basim, and that none of these foreigners that she works with or takes to tourist shops ever touched her. In fact she is eager to guard herself against vice, in spite of the temptations she comes across every day with every man she meets in the streets downtown. If she paid any attention to all the flattering words directed at her, in every ruined building or trash pile you'd find tons of cotton carrying the corpses of her aborted fetuses. She will tell you that foreigners consider her extraordinarily beautiful, despite the fact that, as Basim says, she is average looking. You will tell her that she looks like the actress Hanan Turk, especially in the glimmer of her eyes and her slender build, and her alluring charm as it shows on the screen. But she will tell you she would like it better if you compared her to Angham, since she is delicate and sensitive, and her voice is beautiful and distinctive, and she isn't easily beaten by hard knocks. She'll ask you, "Did you hear her song:"

> *Nothing fancy and nothing to hide,*
> *That's how I live with my heart open wide,*
> *To the whole wide world and the people in it.*
> *I'll call out to my time and say:*
> *I'm all about the young, their hopes and dreams....*

You are cheered by these lyrics, and repeat them, and after you leave her you go buy the album and easily memorize the song. You will remember Nadia saying that western men are more romantic than eastern men: they don't treat women with contempt, and don't suffer from schizophrenia, and they aren't afflicted by guilt after talking with or kissing a foreign woman. "When he loves, he gives everything. Why aren't eastern men that way, like westerners? You're different from them," she tells you. Later, you often go downtown, where you always see Basim walking with a purposeful stride with a westerner; you hope to see Nadia, too, but you're never in luck.

❖

Talaat is responsible for those who befriend foreigners in downtown Cairo. He knows about all their situations, and he is the one who organizes their activities. He is always meeting with them in the al-Bustan coffeeshop, talking with them and trying to solve their problems. He is also friends with most of the tourist police in Cairo, especially the Qasr al-Nil and Pyramids districts. Sometimes he is an informer and a lookout for the police when a foreigner is robbed or murdered. He offered the first tip in the murder case of the French lady killed by one of the unofficial tourist guides. He killed her because she had betrayed him with a Nubian doorman, and because she refused to give him some of the cash he needed for medical treatment for his sick mother, who had been lying in bed for two months in Qasr al-Aini Hospital, waiting her turn for surgery. He is a go-between when a fight breaks out among the unofficial guides, arising from disputes between the amateurs and professionals. The amateurs are students in language programs at university humanities departments and at tourism institutes. They are driven by a desire to befriend foreigners in order to learn their language and practice it, and to examine the neat-and-tidy western mentality. Among the professional guides are those looking to get their daily bread, a rolled cigarette, and a quiet nap from these foreigners. Talaat works from the start of the day until its end, and sits in the coffeeshop at sunset. He has lookouts on the streets downtown, and when a problem comes up, he goes to the police department to vouch for the tour guide's character, and pays the required fees for him. If the guide is arrested with drugs on him, then he brings a lawyer along, in order to persuade the police officer that the drugs were for personal use, not for distribution. He had warned Basim about Nadia, telling him she was young and would cause problems for him. But when Basim got her pregnant, Talaat tried to help her out, and gave her the money she needed for the operation. Then he limited her activities downtown, fearing that she would turn into a prostitute, especially after she fell hard for Basim. He didn't respect Basim, but was afraid of him, not only because of his father's influence and the high-ranking position of his sister's husband with the police, but also because Basim was very familiar with downtown Cairo and drew a lot of customers to the tourist shop that Talaat owned. Basim would get his cut without an argument, and he was known as the cleverest and most consequential man downtown. Basim will tell you to be on your guard about Talaat, since he loves good-looking men, despite being married with three sons. Often you see him sitting alone in the Beautiful View Coffeeshop by Bab al-Luq Square, smoking a sheesha. He notices you and smiles, inviting you to sit down. You answer him in greeting, but keep your distance, remembering Basim's observation about his behavior, even though you claim to have embraced a liberated outlook on life, and let people do what they like.

Talaat will always see you walking with your friends from the American University, but he doesn't talk to you or harass you. He won't bother the foreigners who are walking with you in Talaat Harb Square. He will understand completely that you are capable on your own, and he won't bother you like the amateurs do. You will be amazed by how heavy he is, and marvel at how he carries his giant head on his short neck, but you will like his high spirits and his constant motion.

Autobiography

Basim was the first child in his small family, and the center of its life. His mother studied child psychology as well as music, and she knew how to cultivate his musical taste by playing music for him and training him to sing flawlessly. She also chose toys for him that developed his mental abilities, such as building blocks and construction sets, and books that developed his learning and intelligence as a child. Thus, he read the adventures of Superman and Spiderman, *Samir* children's magazine, and Ladybird children's books. When his sister arrived, less interest was taken in him, and he began acting out more in order to keep getting attention. Then the third and fourth siblings arrived, and interest in him disappeared altogether.

A lot of restrictions were placed on him; he was neglected and his parents didn't talk much to him. They left their old home in the al-Munira district and went to the completely new district of Abbas al-Aqqad. He left behind his close friends in school and felt alone and isolated. His father began to travel more frequently, working on diplomatic negotiations between Egypt and Israel. As for his sister, she was busy with her fiancé, a dedicated police officer. Basim began to feel jealous of him, because she had been very close to him before she became engaged, especially when Basim would fight with his mother, who would avoid him and argue with him for days. She would order him to his room for hours without allowing him to come out, as if she were a jailer. He would cry by himself and call down a curse on her that she would never make the hajj to Mecca. Nevertheless, she began going on hajj every year, as if in defiance of his curse. His sister devoted all her time to her fiancé who became the "officer in love," and neglected her brother. Basim almost went mad because he had been forgotten by everyone—even the lady next door, whom he loved, but couldn't go any further with, since she was so conservative that she wouldn't let him kiss her. He needed every touch of affection and a woman's full embrace. The call of his body and his desire were stronger than any idealized or innocent sentiments that a youth his age might have, so that he became addicted to watching obscene films and bedding girls who were freed from all social and religious constraints. His mother asked him to practice yoga, so that he could be liberated from the tyranny of the body as a means of deliverance from base and earthly ideas. She also asked him to train himself to meditate. Whenever someone, especially children, visited her, she would teach them the principles of yoga and would reward the child who sat quietly without moving for the longest time possible. But meditation is no longer any use to an aroused body and a headstrong desire, especially when he got to know a friend who befriended foreigners, who convinced him that his English wouldn't get any better unless he talked to native speakers. His visits to downtown Cairo grew frequent, and his hobby of talking with foreigners turned into a profession, until he got to know the American woman, Jackie. She was light-skinned, with blue eyes the color of the sky and the waters of the Atlantic Ocean, and an effervescent personality. They rented an apartment together in Manial, and she was madly in love with him. She refused to leave Cairo, unless he came back with her to the United States of America.

It wasn't a shock to his father when Basim announced his relationship with the American girl, since this wasn't the first time Basim was meeting foreigners. It was a nice opportunity for him to leave this country, which had grown too confining for its people, and where the individual had become part of a growing number that had no material or spiritual worth. Thousands of professionals and educated people had moved to the Gulf and most of the government jobs had become a haven for the idle and the marginalized: so why shouldn't he go to America? Egypt had become America's main ally in the Middle East after the Camp David Accords, and it was an opportunity for Basim to steer clear of the Muslim Brotherhood, which he joined, disregarding what his family said, during his summer break, along with his cousin Usama in Alexandria. Instead of coming back to Cairo wearing seawater and a sunburnt face and shoulders, Basim came back bearded and with his jilbab shortened to a little below his knees. His father swore he would divorce his wife if Usama ever entered their house.

No one thought about the fate of this young man in a big, frightening country like the U.S. He left the university without finishing his studies, and left his money in the wallet of this foreign wife. He left behind theater at his university, and left behind the music notes through which he had practiced some pieces, especially on the guitar, and he went to the land of snow: the melting pot of humanity.

❖

You try to help him, Nadir, so you introduce him to your friends who work in television so that he can work as a broadcaster for a children's program, but he fails spectacularly because he doesn't wake up early enough, and because of his western way of life, and his strange clothes, seeing as how he goes to the television studio in the Maspero Building wearing shorts and worn-out sandals. And also because of his failure to obtain a diploma that he could present to the personnel department so that he could have an employment contract drawn up and receive a salary. He will try to make you believe that he is friends with a well-known, older female television personality, and that he has a close relationship with her—that perhaps she is trying to seduce him, or is hoping to marry him, especially since he's regained his vital spirit, and his old shine has come back.

❖

"We've given up hope about fixing Basim." So family members will tell you when they get together on special occasions. They will also say there's nothing to be done about him, that his father is the ultimate reason for the way he is, especially since his mother died, perhaps from pain, or perhaps from grief. After suffering a hemorrhage, she advised him to hold fast to prayer and the Qur'an, since they offer salvation from this ephemeral life. She left him all alone, and he grieved for her, going to the deserts of the Fayoum where her gravesite was. He visits her at night, and plants a henna plant that she had bought before she died from the Spring Flower Show at the al-Urman Garden, after she had had a dream about it. He weeps beside her grave, heedless of the voices of those in torment in the underworld, and of the souls of children that swarm around cemeteries, gathering gifts left there, or of the jinn looking for a body they can possess and yoke themselves to.

❖

When he takes a romantic interest in Manar, a friend of your brother Magid, and then goes with her to her house, he claims that she isn't "respectable," since she let him kiss her and touch sensitive areas of her body, and he comes to tell your brother about what happened. Your brother comes to hate him and kicks him out of his life. You will confront Manar, and she will tell you that Basim is lying, that nothing like that happened, and that she has been alone ever since your brother broke off contact with her because she got married to an engineer, who was later imprisoned for his involvement in burglarizing gold shops in the Ain Shams district. She was suspected of aiding and abetting, and ended up alone, mother to a child asking about her father. She needed someone to listen to her, and make her feel she hadn't been cut off from the world due to wearing the veil and to society's suspicious view of her involvement in the robberies.

You will ask yourself: what's behind Basim's appeal to women? What's the source of his charm and his attractiveness? Are there things in life that keep him busy other than sleeping with women?

Basim will tell you that he is incapable of living without a woman, and that whoever enters the labyrinth of women cannot come out, because they are the spirit of life. Egyptian women, he says, are no good for him anymore, because they are more materialistic than western women: they want a house, children, and power. Love and a husband are the means to get what they want. It has reached the point that he no longer understands the Egyptian mentality of exploitation.

September 11

Basim will call Nadir the moment the World Trade Center towers in New York burst into flames, saying that he's not gloating over the Americans' misfortunes, but divine providence took revenge on his behalf against those who had humiliated him and crushed him, even though he wasn't guilty of anything. He was the one who went to them, bearing innocent love and a breathless infatuation for a people who dominate the world and who had gone to the moon. He himself dreamed of one day flying a rocket that would set him down on other planets at a moderate cost, to make it possible for everyone in the world to behold the wonders of existence and the power of the Creator. He was dazzled by the skyscrapers, the fast trains, and the clean streets, the different kinds of people and their languages—as though the Tower of Babel had come crashing down in the United

States—the unlimited freedom, the minorities and their neighborhoods, whole continents of humanity from different cultures and origins in one nation.

He will talk about the thick smoke produced by the collision, saying that it looks like the nuclear mushroom cloud produced when the United States detonated the atom bomb over Hiroshima and Nagasaki during the Second World War. He will tell you that the moment when the two towers collapsed was the greatest catastrophe to befall the land of dreams. You try to tell him that you saw this scene on Al Jazeera, and on Channel One, and you saw how people ran terrified, as though it was the terrible Day of Judgment.

He will say that this Bin Laden is Saladin, who defeated the Crusaders, and that he plans to read a lot about this man and about the Taliban, these young men who "believed in their Lord, and We increased them in guidance," and that if the Arabs united to bring down this arrogant nation, then Jackie would be brought down, too, forever. Perhaps she will return as part of the captured war-prizes that the new Muslims will take prisoner. Perhaps the time has come to end once and for all the marginalization the Arabs have suffered from in the world, as if they are just a nation of "camels and sands, oil and Bedouin headdresses." You will tell him he shouldn't be too optimistic: who knows what the future holds for us from the United States? He laughs, and tells you that "the future" won't trouble us, since we are their chief allies in the Middle East. Sure, it's possible that Syria or Libya or even Saudi Arabia will be hurt. As for Iraq, it's the golden goose that keeps laying the barrels of oil that keep America's children warm.

Nadir is slow to pass judgment on things and he will sit for hours and hours watching satellite channels—especially Al Jazeera—often seeing the face of Bin Laden as he threatens the United States with annihilation. Nadir will dream of the million dollar reward for apprehending him and turning him over to the Americans. America won't forget to collect old debts, as he calls to mind Basim's imprisonment for the sake of a few paltry dollars. For a long time he will stop writing, doing nothing but watching television and news reports that give him a powerful headache and a heaviness in his eyes when he wakes up. He will lose his will to live, and his laughs will become few and far between, until they disappear altogether. He will say that the present moment with its irrational events is more powerful than any writing, and that literary imagination is incapable of depicting them. Friends advise him to steer clear of politics, and to write about what he likes, but he can't. Hours and hours will be lost to him. He watches scenes of violence and death and bloodshed, as his belief that there is goodness to be found in humanity diminishes. He believes that violence is the religion the world now embraces.

❖

Every time you see Basim walking by the al-Bustan Mall, he enters the internet café and sits for hours talking with Judy, who sends him a photo of a little girl named Aster: he had wanted to name her Salome. You will also see him walking with men younger than him, and when you ask him about them, he tells you they are just some guys and friends from work. Every time he will invite you to go with him on a trip to Sharm al-Sheikh because that's where new things are happening: the president has a big vacation home there; money laundering and normalization with Israel have become big money-makers in that town, as a way to emerge from the nation's economic crisis. Basim will discover that his father owned a piece of land around Taba that had been given to him as a reward, although for what Basim has no idea. His father never told him about it; after Basim's mother died, he sold it in order to marry a girl from the countryside, to ensure that she would stay on and remain devoted to him. Inevitably, Basim will come back from Sharm al-Sheikh, to tell you that he learned how to be a diving instructor, which is a very profitable line of work, since you get paid in dollars. He will invite you to dinner and complain about his father's greed and his excessive love for his unfortunate wife, Naama, who was forced by poverty and need to consent to marry a man her father's age. He will say that his father insists on getting back the amount of money he paid to get Basim out of prison in Boston. Basim will ask you for some cash to buy food for the rabbits and gas for the car, and for dinner. You will feel compelled to agree, because he is your relative, and because he treated you hospitably when you visited him in Boston. Basim's father will avoid having much to do with him, and will shut his door in his son's face, telling him he should rely on himself, and that he can't be supporting a grown man who's pushing forty. He'll tell Basim that he has other things to do in life, and that he's already spent a lot of money on him, from the time he was a small child up to when America let him out of prison, and even after he came back to Cairo. He'll tell him he wants to live in peace with his new wife, and that it wouldn't be right for Basim to live with them in the same house, particularly since Basim threatened to sleep with

159

her one day if his father ever married her and violated the memory of Basim's mother. He will tell Basim that political life is unsettled these days, and that he has to focus on his work; otherwise, he will lose his job. That there is new thinking that has taken hold in the region, especially when it comes to preparing the nation for the next president. He'll tell him that the region is on fire, and needs his full attention, inasmuch as America had goaded the Middle East by invading Iraq and bringing down Saddam's regime. He will tell Basim that the Islamic Jihad movement and its organized campaign of terror necessitated special focus from the Egyptian secret police, so that they could learn about its operations, especially after the United States asked Egypt for complete cooperation in this area in the wake of September 11. Basim will yell at him, saying that even dogs feed their children and tigers feed their young. That there is nothing fatherly about him. That he misses his mother very much, and that spoiled girl of his should be his daughter, not his wife. That the reason his mother died was her intense feelings of jealousy over his behavior and his notorious relationships with disreputable women. That he has made a pact with the devil and the dictator nation. That he hates him because he cooperates with a country that claims to be good, but is the root of evil and hatred in the world. That he won't forgive those unthinking people—they are the reason why his future is ruined and why he is a disgrace to himself and to other people. That the new world order under the leadership of the United States is a big lie: the advanced nations of the west don't believe it, but it's the weak countries that are under threat, and have to obey orders without regard to their people's welfare or dignity.

You will claim the principle of tolerance, and tell Basim that there are good people in the United States and the west who don't deserve all this rage coming from him. You will tell him that people there are more than just the American Congress and the European Union. The people who set policies are a few individuals acting according to a master plan similar to Freemasonry that seeks to achieve domination and an international balance of power. That the American people have no power, just like us Arabs: they chase after their daily bread and a peaceful life for themselves. But he objects, saying that this kind of talk is nonsense: there is a very high level of education in the United States, and the masses can't be laughed off the way they are in this half-illiterate society. You tell him he should remember the smiles he received from children and old people, or the human moments he had with average people in their everyday dealings, such as when one of them invites you to lunch or to have a cup of coffee, or asks how you're feeling if you seem upset. Or when you enter a library and the librarian helps you get a book or lets you wander at your leisure without bothering you. Or when a local stands with you at the entrance to the subway, so he can look at the map and show you where you need to go when you're lost, or when someone gives you a lift in his car when you miss the bus to get you to where you want to go. This is humanity, these are the memories that you bring back with you from your time away from home. It's not exclusively evil, because evil is found in your nation, too. When he hears these words, he will grow annoyed, until he is on the verge of tears, and he leaves you blaming yourself, as you recall what things were like for you, and what you did in Boston when you visited him.

He will tell you that he should begin again, that life isn't over yet, that failure is a part of existence and that he has a lot of talents he should be taking advantage of. Even if you don't start off wealthy, there are a lot of TV programs now that are concerned with talented people, like *Star Academy*, and *Art Studio*. There is also private music producing—why doesn't he sell the car and put out a song that he can distribute himself to private satellite stations? You are absolutely certain that he will succeed due to his fine voice and his good looks. He dreams big and begins singing, but he gets depressed again, and then comes to you with the surprising news that he wants to act. Now he is seeing a girl called Naha who is a screenwriting student at the Cinema Institute. She is captivated by him, and feels that his life would make a great full-length feature film that young people should see. She is infatuated with the world and the milieu he inhabits, and with the humble apartment in which he lives. The view of the vast wasteland surrounding his house is paradise, as far as she's concerned. She begins to write the first scenes for the movie, and what happened to him in prison. He helps her write the dialogue. She uses him as a model for a short film she makes to persuade the Cinema Institute to accept her project. The film is based on a short story by Garcia Marquez. Not long into their relationship, she starts coming to him at midnight, saying that she had had a fight with her mother over her mother's bad treatment of her father, who then left the house for several days. Her parents fought because her father still thinks about the world like an old socialist. He attends panel discussions held by the al-Tagammu Party, and sits for hours at cafés writing sharply critical articles about the government for opposition newspapers like *al-Arabi al-nasseri*, as well as papers that nobody reads and that don't pay him anything. He joins strikes and fasts in solidarity on every occasion when students or the people protest against Israel or America. He almost died of hunger when he took part in a sit-in at the Lawyers' Syndicate when America decided to invade Iraq. He brags that Hamdin Sabbahi was his companion at this sit-in. Sabbahi came out of it a hero, while her father was released to enter the hospital, and suffered from the effects of dehydration for several months. It was Naha who rescued the books he had kept for years, such as *Das Kapital* by Marx, *The Communist Manifesto*, some writings by Roger Garaudy, and the memoirs of Muhammad al-Jundi, especially the piece called *Children's Story*, from being burned when her mother had a fight with her father one day and set fire to his library, until Naha brought the books to Basim's house. Basim reads all the books from cover to cover, but he still tells her that it's the dollar, not the ruble, that rules the world now. And that concepts like "social justice," "the elimination of class differences," and "the rights of workers," or economic questions like the relationship between the true value of something and its surplus-value, are completely alien to the average subjugated man in a world ruled by the globalization movement, and devoid of a social safety net.

She says, while crying on his shoulder one evening and gazing distractedly into the weak light cast from the lamp, that her mother treats her like a prostitute because of her independent way of life, even though it was her mother who encouraged her to enter the Cinema Institute, because she had failed to become an actress, or even a writer, herself. Oftentimes she prevents her from going out by soaking her clothes in water on the pretext of washing them. As a result, she is forced to wear the same winter coat for several days on end, while wearing clothes that are too light for winter underneath it. A lot of times she hates her mother, and wishes she were dead. If it weren't for her younger brothers, she would have left for somewhere else. She doesn't much believe the Prophet's saying that "Paradise lies at the feet of mothers"—in fact, sometimes Hell lies at their feet. It was her mother who taught her to borrow so much from her friends, to the point of exploiting them. If it weren't for her bashful face and her natural innocence, people would have treated her more harshly. She sometimes feels ashamed by her mother's presence in her life, and wonders why her father, such a simple man, got involved with this cruel woman who couldn't care less whether her daughter was happy in life or not.

She will say that her mother also had a miserable childhood, since she never knew a father's affection, and eloped with the first man who asked her to marry him. And that, after the wedding night, she decided to take revenge on all men, just like her father. Her mother stopped distinguishing between her children and men, and became an expert in torturing us and them, she says. The sun of love set on their house long ago, she says, and she never saw her mother kiss her father, as though he were a close blood-relative or else a complete stranger to her. She wondered at how she came into the world if this was how they behaved in bed, and in life. This behavior on her mother's part soured her on life and everything in it, and she began to want to hurt herself in order to get back at her. Other times, she wanted to return to her father's loins and swim there, being nothing other than an X-chromosome that carries no traits, in a state of eternal non-existence, unbreathed-upon by the spirit of God. At other times, she felt that she wanted to enter her mother's womb again in order to flee from this cruel world. She imagines that her mother will want to take her back and make up to her the affection she never had. Basim told her that she suffers from an Electra complex and that she needs to get rid of this feeling, or otherwise she will go mad.

She understood that her mother wasn't happy, because she was the one providing for the home while her father searched for social justice outside it and neglected his work. Naha became confused and didn't know what to do until she met Basim in the al-Hurreya Coffeehouse, and he ordered her a coffee. Then she shared a glass of beer with him—the only thing he could afford to buy. Then he invited her to his house, and she went. She told him that the al-Hurreya Coffeehouse is the meeting place of most of those who are looking to find something they can be serious about, either in art or in life. Her chance came to her when she got to know him.

He will tell you that her chance of success is slim, since she doesn't have someone to support her in this business. Talent by itself isn't enough. She is shy and incapable of degrading herself, since she can't give herself to a man without love. For her, love is not only a physical relationship that frees the body of its blocked fluids. Rather, it is an existential voyage. Her love is pure and intense. She despises infidelity the way she hates unbelief. Jealousy is a sickness she will never be free of. She warned Basim that she might kill him if he got close to another woman.

Naha came over, and told him, "Abd al-Halim, the one you listen to? Forget about him. Artists that authority approves of are always popular, but they never say anything important." Then she opened her bag and took out a cassette tape, saying, "Surprise!" She leaned over to pop the cassette into the stereo. Basim saw her from behind and felt desire for her. "Shaykh Imam!" she said gleefully. "Songs and issues, fun and revolution. I stole this tape from my mother, who was a friend of Ahmad Fuad Negm. She used to go with him to the Hosh Adam neighborhood. Once, my father caught her there, lying on the mat. She was drunk and half-asleep, as if she had taken opium, and next to her was a man kissing her neck. He flew into a rage and poured a cup of tea over her head."

Basim was listening to her without interest, and was busy trying to make out what Shaykh Imam was singing, like the song "Shurm Burm," which was about Zionist penetration into the Middle East; or his mockery of Sadat's sophistication and the prayer-bump on his forehead in his song "Ahu;" and the double-entendres in "The Farmgirl's Dough." He listened to the tape until the end. She was delighted, as if she had given him a treasure and expected that this revolutionary singer would have an effect on him, but he didn't show much interest. "His time has passed," he said. "We need someone to tell us about the present. Why do we love the past and make giants of the dead?" Naha lit a cigarette and leaned against him, then stretched out her legs. She reclined her head on his shoulder, then her mouth began to water, and she felt her cheeks grow warm. She pressed against his lips, kissing them softly, and he took her lips between his. Then after pulling back, she whispered, "I love you. You're the one I need in this world." He drew her forcefully to his chest, with his eyes closed and said in a whisper, "I need you too. I need the whole world beside me."

❖

Naha will say, "Let's go to the La Chesa Restaurant together, have some gateaux and drink cappuccino. We'll listen to some light music, especially on a summer day like this when the air is hot and stifling with Central Security forces outside guarding the al-Ahly Bank and the synagogue. We'll sit in cool air thanks to the air conditioning. We'll sit for hours and make small talk about life and films. There's always a famous director sitting there, one of my teachers at the Institute, but he never invites me to sit with him, even though one of my friends said that he's dying to get to know me. He told her I would be a sex-symbol —just imagine that! Even though my friends say I'm only right for completely innocent roles, like Fatin Hamama before she starred 'Sleepless.'

"I'm not suited to being an actress, because I'm afraid of facing people," she added. "It happens when I go into cafés downtown: I get confused and my feet trip themselves up, like I'm a child just learning to walk. Or like I've been sick for many months. I can feel people's eyes examining me, like x-rays penetrating my bones. So I wear a mask of indifference and head for the table I want. I don't pay attention to anyone. I know that my body isn't beautiful, and that I am heavier than I should be. If it weren't for the whiteness of my skin, men wouldn't like me: Arab men love women with soft, white skin. But I will go on a strict diet to lose weight; I'll try

167

a diet of apples and honey. It's hard to do because apples are expensive these days, but I'll try. If the diet doesn't work, I'll try liposuction, especially on my behind. I want to wear jeans without worrying about it, and wear evening dresses without looking like a professional dancer or a call-girl.

"I love the al-Hurreya Coffeehouse when daylight fills it between midday and afternoon," she said, "when it's quiet and clean and the sun gently advances across the floor. I drink my coffee and read a little or write a scene for my new film, and watch the passersby from behind the glass without them noticing me. It's beautiful to watch people secretly without their noticing that they're being observed. You feel you're being a voyeur, that you're doing something demeaning.

"My mother always does that. She keeps an eye on me and examines my sanitary pads. She makes a point of looking at my nipples to check their color, afraid that she might be surprised one day by me coming to her and telling her that I'm pregnant."

"What kind of sanitary pads do you use?" Basim said, talking like a radio announcer. "Do they have wings?"

"What did you say, you rude person?" she answered, while punching him on the shoulder.

"Let's fly away together on them!" he said, embracing her, as they laughed. Some time later, Basim said, "Aren't you fed up with this aimless life spent among the cafés? Don't you dream of settling down like every other Egyptian woman? A place to live, a house, children?"

"All that's changed. It's no longer the ambition of young women now, now that everything is different: a woman is no longer just a man's sweetheart, but his competitor. Despite that, she wants money, a lover, and a husband."

168

Then she added, as she got closer to him, "My ambition isn't to be rich; it's art, which is immortality. I know that you will make me immortal with your life's story and your love." Then she wept in pain, as though she had lost something dear to her.

❖

Basim will say that Naha was similar to him in a lot of respects, that she was very smart, that her sentiments were noble and very good-hearted, like kindly grandmothers, and that people like her are too good for this world. He will say that she was going to introduce him to Dawood Abd al-Sayid or Khalid Yusef or Hani Khalifa, so that they could make a star out of him, and that life had wronged her the way it had wronged him.

He will say that he wouldn't have known about Guevara or Fidel Castro if it hadn't been for her, although their images were widespread in Boston as symbols of independence and defense of the rights of peoples whom America had subjugated, especially Vietnam and Cuba. She once gave him a T-shirt that had a picture of Guevara on it that was the talk of downtown Cairo for a week. He thinks about putting up a picture of Guevara on one of the walls in his room, in order to remind himself that Guevara was a sacrificial lamb, just like him. He fully understands that he will die a martyr or a casualty. True, he is not fighting any kind of corruption in politics or society, but he is a martyr in this life that so often wrongs the completely innocent via fate, in the same way that dictatorial countries with their tyranny kill the freedom of small nations to live the way they want to. You will tell him that he is a victim of women and of his own character. But we

169

all have our desires, so we're all martyrs. He begins drawing a picture of Guevara, although you advise him to buy the printed portrait, since it's available everywhere. He doesn't believe he's become like da Vinci yet, because he is still at the beginning of his life as an artist.

After several days, he will come and give you another strange picture of Guevara, as he exhorts the Cuban people to fight injustice through guerilla warfare. He will say that this is a gift for your birthday, and you tell him that Guevara died almost on the day you were born.

Basim is distressed and says that his relationship with Naha didn't last long and that he didn't lose her only because of the wild girl Nadia who began to threaten him with public disgrace and threatened to haul him to court on a paternity claim. Rather, it was because Naha sponged off of him on numerous occasions, showing up at his house uninvited, and because of her jealousy of foreign women: several times she banged on the door until she woke the neighbors, and threatened that if he didn't open up, she would throw herself off the roof of the building, and then they would toss him in prison. She would make him regret it his entire life. He knew she was crazy and had an unstable personality. Women like that are dangerous: even if they are creative, the idea of suicide always dwells in their minds and clings to their souls like perfume. She also was not entirely clean, and used to leave her underwear on the washbasin. She didn't respect the sanctity of her monthly periods, as though she wanted to provoke him. She wasn't satisfied with kissing, although she was still a virgin, and he was afraid of going too far with her. He suspected that she was paranoid, and that she wouldn't end up making the film. He also suspected she suffered from a father complex, since he saw her on several occasions sitting in the company of old men in restaurants all over downtown, like the Grillon and Estoril. He kicked her out of his house forever when he came out of the bathroom and found her strangling the rabbits that Judy had bought to assuage his loneliness while she was away in Canada. She had also made a point of defacing the drawings done by Ophelia, the Austrian girl whom Basim had welcomed into his home for a month when she rented a room in his apartment. She had become enchanted with Egypt, so much so that she drew a lot of sketches from nature, as well as abstract shapes in various shades of blue, mixed with yellow. When Naha defaced Ophelia's drawings, Basim kicked her out of his life forever, and to this day, she has neither written nor directed a film.

❖

You remembered that on the evening you got engaged, you invited Basim, whose father had turned his back on him, to stay the night at your house beside the wide expanse of Lake Qarun, where you held a big party to celebrate getting the woman you loved at first sight. You said, the way they say it in songs: *She is the one who will make me happy in my life*. She looked like the old girlfriend who had left you and married another man whom you couldn't hate because he was your friend. Without meaning to, she succeeded in being your muse when she failed to be your partner in life. She became your inspiration for frustration and personal regret, and you always evoke her in everything you write. With Hosna, you wanted to forget a love that had lasted more than ten years, and which you couldn't expel from within you. When you met Hosna, you became entranced by her, incapable of staying away from her, and after a few weeks, she became all women, and all humanity, and all stories.

You invited Basim, and he came. You noticed him among the invited guests, wearing a suit that wasn't right for his age or his slim frame. He appears stressed. Then you left everyone at the party, and celebrated with her on the lakeshore, holding her to your heart. She embraces you as if she wanted to inject you into her, so that you course through her veins. You embrace her, and leave her, drunk on a feeling you've never before savored. She feels it, and your feeling of intoxication grows, and you both run to the rhythm of the lake's gentle waves, which delicately and affectionately hugs the shore and the sands. You look at the lake, as though it were a dream with the color of her pink engagement dress. You touch her lips as though you are imbibing from the rivers of honey and nectar in paradise.

When you return to the house, you find Basim sitting with your niece Zahra, whom adolescence had left mature in body only. She appeared embarrassed when you opened the door, and only the two of them were in the entrance parlor: your mother is asleep and your brother Magid went to the bar to drink, in order to forget that you threw yourself into the arms of a family unworthy of your talents and social status, and to forget that the hick girl was able to tie you down, using your unsatisfied urges as her rope. You stare daggers at Basim, and tell Zahra to go inside to sleep. He claims that the two of them were staying up watching TV, and nothing else. But you have doubts about what he's telling you, and imagine that what he did with Nadia, he was doing with Zahra, and you get angry. You are stirred up, and you kick him out of your house into the early morning, and you see him walking away by himself. You know for sure he will walk all the way to Nasr City because he has no cash on him, and you regret that you were so harsh. You want to call him, and ask him to come inside. After a few minutes, you see Zahra wearing a new set of clothes. She tells you she has lectures at the university, and has to go. You and she have a fight, and she tells you you're delusional and paranoid, and you almost end up hitting her. You watch from the balcony as you see her walking in the opposite direction; but you imagine them walking together in the quiet, tree-lined streets of Maadi, their hands and spirits entwined.

❖

Basim will pay no attention to Nadir at all, and won't ask himself if the woman that Nadir married recently is making him happy or not, or whether there are satisfactions to be had from her presence in his life. Basim never gets tired of talking about himself and Nadir never gets bored of looking at him and listening to him. Nadir's life will start to go into decline, as his relationship with his wife approaches the abyss. Perhaps his love for writing has become his preoccupation, or perhaps the imagined world has become much more beautiful than the real world, so that he becomes detached from it and unhappy with his life, even with the woman who is supposed to be closest to him. Boredom will eat away at him as he is afflicted by nervous tension, perhaps even neurosis. He will have a lot of fights with his wife, and will give serious thought to separating from her, because she goes on without realizing how much he is suffering. He will feel that she is only concerned with her own feelings and her needs for love and possession, oblivious to Nadir's sensitive soul. He goes out a lot and crosses paths with a great number of people, throwing himself into experiences that he had been afraid of for so long, and that he had denied himself. He will take risks with people, with words and actions, and experience for himself all ways of life. He will walk a lot in the streets, looking at the faces of passersby, and at the street vendors. He will stare suspiciously at the entrances of old buildings, contemplating the architectural form of their walls and hoping to go inside them, especially the dark ones. He will knock at the doors of the building door-keepers, to talk with them. He will make friends with everyone who sits next to him on the microbus or subway. He will give his phone number to large numbers of women and men, and make them believe that he wants to be their friend, or even to have intimate relationships with them. When they call him, he won't answer the phone, and even if he sees them again in the street, he won't remember them, will ignore them, and won't talk to them. He will leave them totally confused, claiming to be Basim, although he is actually Nadir.

❖

Basim will introduce you to some of his freelance tour-guide friends, and tell you that they are a world unto themselves, and that behind every one of them is an exciting and magical reality. So you ask him, did you see the movie *Romantica*? The title astonishes him. After he introduces you to his friend Salah and tells you, "He is the best guy in downtown Cairo," and that his father is the biggest dealer in authentic papyrus

174

paper—not banana paper—Salah insists you visit his private papyrus showroom on Talaat Harb Street. You step inside the building, and it's like you're entering the King's Chamber in the Great Pyramid: a long, subterranean passageway leads you to a basement with a small room full of pharaonic illustrations of various shapes and colors, as if they were from the workshops of the pharaohs themselves. Salah's father talks about his love for this business, its secrets, and how to recognize authentic sheets of papyrus and imitations. Then, after he begins to trust you, he looks into your eyes a good deal, touches your warm hands time to time, and evinces a strong interest in you. Then he whispers, in breaths redolent of coffee and opium, that he has papyrus sheets that are five thousand years old, bearing commandments found in the "Book of the Dead." He whispers that he stole them during his work in the former Antique-Khana Museum in the 1950s, during the excavation of the gravesite of the pharaoh Khufu in the Nazlet al-Samman area. He tells you that he was dismissed from his work for stealing these papers, and would have gone to prison if not for the fact that he had smuggled them out to his relatives in the Falaqa district in Damanhur al-Buheira—and also because a lot of the world's presidents and ministers of culture are his friends: they visit him whenever they get an opportunity. You will tell Salah's father about the taxi driver who showed you a statue of Nefertari that he was planning to sell to one of the rich people at the American University in Cairo, when you mentioned to him that you were studying there. Salah's father's face will turn serious as he tells you that he doesn't do business in idols or mummies, and that papyrus sheets are the really valuable treasure.

As for Salah, you see him correcting some shading for a Korean girl who is tracing the head of Cleopatra in various colors. He puts some of the red pigment on her lip to make her look like a real beauty. Salah will talk to you a lot in English, and you will try to ignore him when you see him. You will get have a falling-out with him when Basim tells you that Salah hates you because you felt up his girlfriend while she was sitting between the two of you in the subway, and you stuck your fingers between her thighs with the aim of arousing her. You defend yourself, telling him, He's crazy—he's out of mind!" He agrees with you and says that Salah is popping pills, but you don't understand. He will tell you that he refuses to drop Salah as a friend since he isn't aggressive and he doesn't rob foreigners or rip them off—he only has a nice time with them. Salah's father keeps him supplied with everything he needs, and Salah often passes women on to him. He's a good guy in all senses of the word, and really knows what a friend is entitled to.

❖

"Don't blame Basim," your brother Magid said. "At least he knows what he's doing. But you're a failure in everything. Especially with women."

What would it mean to be successful? you ask yourself.

You've done everything in your power to succeed. You put in the effort and studied, and you avoided all activities that might waste your time and distract you from the goal laid out for you. You would see people and get along well with them; you would be on close terms with them, but you didn't have the time to get to know them better. It's like were sitting next to them on a train: when you reach the end of the trip, everyone goes his own way. As if the fates worked to arrange things so that you could make myself what you are, but was it really you who made yourself what you are? After God, your mother and father and your sister are the ones who molded you. They gave and didn't expect anything in return. They stayed up at night working, while you were sitting in your room reading books that breathe with the spirit and ideas of those who are dead and gone. They toiled and slaved away and wore out their health, while you were enjoying your lectures, and your circuit of seminars and libraries. You look down on them, and on their jobs. You accuse them of being ignorant and backward and being blind to what is truly valuable.

Magid your brother asks you, "Don't you make any profit from art?" "Art is for art's sake," you reply. He tells you to show more enthusiasm for life and the people in it, and asks you to treat them like flesh and blood, not like ideas and stories that you are eager to find out about so you can record them in your notebooks. Your brothers are real and their love for you is real. But you have a selfishness in you and you call it art.

What have you done for them? And what have you given them? Did you ask them to relax a little so that you can assume responsibility, and pay back a little of what you owe them? You're a writer and a university lecturer—you could market yourself for a lot of money these days, but you're a shirker and a slacker. You feed off their livelihoods and call yourself an artist. So get out of the cocoon, dust yourself off, and be a real individual, before it's too late. Take the blindfold off, and look at life with an experienced eye. Make your mark, and don't retreat from the fight before it's over. Take a stance

177

and don't let anyone accuse you of having a negative attitude. Did you love Nadia? Did she rule your emotions—this girl who fanned the flames of love in you?

You flee from your wife to her. You claim she has more life and humanity in her than the woman you were dazzled by when you first saw her. Instead, you find yourself drowning in primitive lust and instinct until you are sated. Then you asked if you could pray, and you left her on the bed, in her pink room, where you pray . . . because you're there with her, and ejaculating into her "holy of holies." What happened and where did your infatuation with your wife go? Can a man turn away from a woman he once desired and asked to marry him? Or are boredom and falling for someone else a reason to split up? You say that your wife doesn't share your interests, but you were the one who kept her away from your creative writing, because she became a menace: she scrutinizes your female characters and longs to find out who this woman is that you are always writing about in your stories.

Then Nadia comes and creates a new world for you, one that appears in force on your horizon, then flickers out sometimes.

When you meet women and fall in love with them, when you let them occupy a vast expanse of your thoughts and imagination, as you weave dreams for an eternal life with them—do they all have love and a protective friendship within them that shelters you both? Yes, you've crossed paths with a lot of women, but you never took the initiative to have any of them be your permanent partner. Even if we assume that a relationship is real and will last forever, for some reason you have doubts about women and their sincerity toward you. You say they can't be trusted, and that they change men the way they change their stockings, not only the men they associate with, but the ones they merely think about or lust after. The first time you had the boldness to say that, and explain it to a woman, she asked you, "Don't men lust after women, even if just by looking at them? Why do you have a poor opinion of women and say they're not allowed to do that? Cherchez la femme," she said; perhaps your first experience with women is the reason. When you told her, "I have intimate, positive relationships," she said, "Could it be you're telling me a little bit about your mother?" You found yourself unable to respond. She looked at you for a long time and then said, "Mothers are men's secret lovers." Then she asked, "Did you read *Sons and Lovers* by D.H. Lawrence? Where the relationship of the mother, Madame Muriel, with her sons was the only obstacle to their development, psychologically and sexually? Her son Paul couldn't perform physically with a woman until after his mother died."

"Why do you always force lust into your argument?" you asked. "Are you looking to get into a relationship with me?" This was the first time you talked in a forthright and sexually frank way with a woman who was known for her culture and knowledge, as she drank beer amid a group of educated people.

So admit it: you are afraid of desire. Admit that your ideal is chastity and abstinence, or perhaps a lot of things you can't detect in yourself. You've always lived with the Messiah as your ideal and Joseph is your exemplar of purity, but you seem to have forgotten that they were prophets: they're not completely human; they're luminous.

You tell yourself you want a woman to be an innocent

179

young thing, and when you find her you blame yourself, saying, I don't love ignorant women who have no experience in life or in conversation. You say, I want an independent woman who challenges the masculinity within me, and who embodies the legend of Isis. Women with little experience are easy to seduce, you say, and men exploit their naivete to get what they want.

❖

You are filled with senseless drivel and mad ideas, Nadir. Your despair grows until it becomes as large as oceans, as dry land recedes from them. In despair, you try to piece together what has broken and crumbled into fragments within you. Terror fills you until you are inundated by it, leaving no opening for security and peace of mind to slip through. Your eyes wander and can't settle on anything, and your laughter is followed by an anxious silence that betrays a greater crisis, one that smothers all the vitality within you. So do without and perhaps you will be pure. Pray and perhaps you will understand or reach the hidden truth within you.

Your inner voice says go outside yourself and contemplate the world around you. Reflection and meditation are the foundations by which man comes to know himself, and to reach his higher self.

Why are you preoccupied with yourself? You didn't create yourself, so why plumb the depths so much you need a psychiatrist?

A psychiatrist again. The tranquilizers that almost killed you that time you took more than the prescribed dose by mistake, when you read "5 milligrams" as "25 milligrams." Your heart almost stopped, and your pulse slowed down abnormally. You began staring off into space, and collapsed on the bed, lying stretched out all night long, a rigid corpse incapable of movement. You were only rescued by your sister, who came in to ask you for some money and noticed you weren't breathing. She woke the entire house with a single scream, and brought you into the bathroom in order to make you vomit, believing that you had attempted suicide. But your stomach was empty. Long nights of suspicion, and several days of trying to get yourself back to normal. Long treatment sessions, and a doctor who said that it's not a crime to acknowledge what you did—in fact, it's the only correct path to psychological health. Friends fall away from you because of your disturbed state, and your inability to understand and help them. You talk well with them about things they're familiar with, and perhaps what they're not familiar with, then you flee at the first real test of the meaning of friendship.

You say that darkness is spreading its tentacles inside you, that your light died out a long time ago, and that the eclipse of your spirit isn't something you've chosen. You say that you're trying to be happy, but can't. You have closed off your senses to the point that you've been thinking a lot about suicide these days. Your life has become meaningless, and your body is wasting away from the pernicious effects of decline, in the expectation that it will dwindle away to nothing, even if you were to throw your body under an express train or under a woman whose aim is to seduce men.

You say, "I'm trying to get a view of my reality, so that I can hold onto my friends, if only a little, so that I can make them happy—they like that. And if I feel isolated and disconnected, well, those feelings are what I deserve to have coming to me."

181

Hours later, you are shedding copious tears. You burst out crying, inundating the place and everyone there. Minutes of happiness, and long hours of loneliness. You want to know what is real, and you ask questions about what you really are, and what the universe is in its essence. You return without satisfactory answers. There is a deep-seated faith within you, but on the level of rituals, you aren't able to commit yourself. You want to understand your body and your soul. You want to know what it means to be a person, and what it means to be a man who is popular with others, a man who can enter a woman's world and possess her, and bind her essence to his on a journey that perhaps will last until life ends.

The psychiatrist says, "You don't need medication, the problem is inside you, not in your consciousness. You are 100 percent normal. Try to live without becoming absorbed in yourself. Insanity means entering into what lies beyond things. Your being wants to be some kind of philosopher as well a normal person, which is something else entirely. Thinking about existence is the greatest human enigma." If only things would reveal themselves and be made clear, and if only people perceived that you are harboring within you broken places that you weren't responsible for, and that it wasn't you who chose to make yourself seem too ungainly and repulsive, the way you appear to yourself sometimes.

Since you left her, you are no longer the way you were, as if she took you with her to her world.

❖

Nadir will feel afraid and have misgivings about everything, and it will grow to take over his life for several days, as he sits in Sufi *zikr* circles in the Sayyidna Hussein

182

Mosque, and wanders around the Gamaliya district. He will read Naguib Mahfouz's *Cairo Trilogy*, then Gamal al-Ghitani's *The Illuminations*, and Bahaa Taher's *Love in Exile*. Then he will go back to reading Kafka and Dostoevsky, and overlook James Joyce completely. He will tell his students, "We want to understand the world—we don't want to make it more puzzling, the way Joyce did." Nadir will leave his wife alone with his mother for several days, despite the fetus growing inside her. Then he will ask her to abort it, because he doesn't want to continue with her beyond than they already have. He claims that the reality of their love ended in the first days of marriage, and that the idea of begetting children in this world is a farcical notion he wants no part of. Her lips will form the word *crazy*, but she won't utter it, perhaps because she loves him, or perhaps because she knows that it's no use. He will go again to the psychiatrist, who will give him Xanax to relieve this condition of his. Because he has to go on, he has to teach, he has to sleep with his wife. He has to continue following the newscasts, and what the United States will do in Afghanistan, and then Iraq, in its war on terror.

❖

Nadir will grow more downcast, and will often go to see Basim, as if in a daze. He will drink beer with him after the Stella bar closes up for the night, and after his friends, writers of prose poetry, disown him. Fathi Abdalla and Hasan Khadr will tell him, "Do like we do: we write poetry in order to rebel against the current situation. We write prose poetry that falls outside the recognized categories, in the exact same

183

way that we in Egypt and the greater Arab world fall between the cracks.

You will be very agitated when the United States makes its decision to declare war on Iraq, and you will go to a demonstration with your writer and student friends, and your novelist friend, whose novel was about someone competing against the nightclubs of the authorities, will be beaten. Your friend Shirin will be put in prison for a few hours before being released, so that people say about her afterward that she has become a big shot, but you see her several times after that, broken and devastated. She's not talking about courage or boldness the way she used to. You will lose faith in the concept of democracy and the justice of the west, and the utopian ideas you spent your life believing in, and which you teach to students, as you see millions of people coming out in demonstrations to stop the aggression facing Iraq from all sides. You will see them on Euronews, BBC, Al Jazeera, and Nile News. The masses will founder as the opposition movement dies with the blast of acid water hoses and tear-gas bombs. With your own eyes, you will see the fall of Baghdad and see the Mongols treading on paintings and sacred books as they cross the Euphrates.

❖

Whenever you meet Basim you find him talking about his financial crisis, and his desire to make some money. You see him sometimes with his head shaved like a neo-Nazi, or letting his hair grow for months on end like a hippie. He talks about his mother a lot, especially after his father remarries.

He says that he misses her a lot: she died unhappy. True, she was a believer, but she suffered very much from her illness, and there was nothing he could do for her. The only thing in life that his despicable father takes an interest in is a meal he can fill his belly with, and a woman he can use to relieve himself of his needs. Basim will tell you that he acts like a nice guy around his father, who lends him cash when he has a nice chick with him, whom he's getting dollars from. You will grow bored of his repeated talk, and tell him, "Why don't you yell at your father, or even kill him, and make it easy on yourself? You are really annoyed by his wishy-washiness and his lack of self-respect, and by people's lack of respect for him. Your mother tells you, "I treat him with respect for the sake of his mother, who was my friend. She and I went on the hajj and umra together. All her life she didn't do wrong by anyone: she only wanted to protect herself from the problems of this complicated world. She had a right to do what she did." Then she recites the Fatiha, and says, "What did I get by opening myself up to the world? I didn't save up anything for myself: it was all for you and your brothers." You tell her that happiness is in giving and in being satisfied. You and she are very attached to each other, and you don't make her angry. You will try to stay close to her, especially after your wife leaves the house. Basim will accuse you of suffering from a Caligula complex and, laughing heartily, you will tell him that he suffers from an Electra complex.

A lot of times, you are hard pressed to stop and greet him, as you see him daily in the downtown area with people you don't know, people you are completely repulsed by because they are deformed. You will see him staggering down the street, high on drugs, and you will be embarrassed to say hello to him, as you walk alone or with friends. He will do that too, and won't approach you unless you approach him. Perhaps you greet him warmly and embrace him, because he is your blood-relative or because he is more than just a friend who has lost his way, a friend you are losing completely, while you claim a specious wisdom and knowledge for yourself. It isn't an acknowledgment of you, but of the diploma hanging on the walls and the papers you keep as proof of your accomplishment. You will tell yourself, I consider him "a friend crisis," like the "wife crisis," you got involved in. You are always a man of crises you create for yourself, after you acknowledge a reality about yourself, or confront people. Just like a woman you once fell in love with, and whom you still love: you meet her all the time without confessing it to her, and by not confessing it, she remains the unattainable woman and you remain the problem man when it comes to her.

❖

You suspect Basim of lying. "How did you let yourself be seduced into doing that to poor, defenseless Nadia?" you ask him. You despise him even more when he tells you that she was a virgin the first time he slept with her, and that he was happy about the feeling that gave him. "Didn't any feelings of guilt come over you?" you ask him. Wouldn't you be worried if that happened to your sister? "She loved it," he says. "And my sister is the wife of a police officer, and she does what she likes. We should be liberated from the body, so our minds can be free." You think about that a lot. You ask yourself, "Are you so different from all these men that your first kiss was with your wife? That you weren't able to discover women except through a legally sanctioned relation-

186

ship? It got to the point that you felt you didn't understand what a woman was, or what sex was, and so you became depressed and lonely. The desires of adolescence tempted you to tease girls, and you made sexual innuendos to the point of being vulgar, so that the more reserved girls refused to have anything to do with you. A friend tells you you've been struck by the voraciousness of delayed desire, but despite that, you still ask about Nadia, and feel some sympathy for her, because of the bitterness of what she went through, and the abortion. "How will she go through life with a soul that has killed the first baby she had with a father who wasn't Basim?" you will ask yourself, "Who was the sympathetic doctor who felt affection for her, and laid aside questions of right and wrong and sex outside of marriage, as he picked up the forceps and scraped the fetus out of the uterus? Who was the nurse who got rid of this fetus, which perhaps carried both Basim and Nadia's traits, without asking for some cash, so she could take care of the disgrace of this girl as she lay with her legs open wide in front of this elderly doctor?"

❖

You will see Basim as you stand in front of Cinema Metro reading the posters for the new film *Gangs of New York*. You cross the street and see him buying ice cream from the Mandarine Koueider pastry shop. "Ice cream in winter?" you ask him. "It's not for me," he replies. "It's for the French chick. We have to pamper women," he says, "so that they will let us enjoy them." He invites you to his apartment to have tea and some food, so you slip over to #42 on Talaat Harb Street. You read on its entrance "Property of the Egyptian Insurance

Company." You and he walk up the winding staircase. You enter the apartment and feel alone. The ceilings are high, and there is no furniture in the apartment. You sense the smell of exile in its darkened corners. Then he opens the door to his room, and you see light after the darkness. You see her. She quietly welcomes you as he begins making introductions. He mentions your cultured status, exaggerating quite a bit, and it embarrasses you. He talks about your visit to Paris and brags that one day he will be a protagonist in one of your stories. Lucine laughs, and tells you that she is studying Arabic and Egyptology, and that Basim has been very helpful for her. He made her read the novel *The Tent* by Miral al-Tahawy, which helped her understand the situation in which Arab women now find themselves. You are amazed by her incorrect reading of the novel. She says that Basim always accompanies her on trips to visit the Mosque of 'Amr ibn al-'As, which she takes as a model for the development of Egyptian Islamic architecture. She talks about how he made it very easy for her when it came to bureaucratic matters. She leans against him flirtatiously and gives him a kiss. Lucine is white-skinned with a slightly plump body. Later, you find out that she is pregnant, and that she wants to keep the child. Around her neck she wears an Arab shawl, which looks like the one Yasir Arafat used to wear on his shoulders as a sign of Palestinian identity. She brings tea with mint and Basim sits down. He picks up the guitar and began to play "Inta Umri." He stops when she signals him to. Then she gets up and puts on the song "Away from You, My Life is Torment." She says she always goes to the Kawkab al-Sharq Coffeeshop on Emad al-Din Street, and asks the waiter to play this song for her because she loves it so much, especially when

Umm Kulthum sighs and sings, "Passion—ahhhh—from passion . . . ." The song has a sadness and mysticism in it that makes her think of an impossible love, and calls to prayer, and the bells of ancient churches she'd been to in the Middle East. She says she is enchanted by the intimate back-and-forth between the qanun and the violin.

"Baligh Hamdi is the product of Egyptian culture," she added, "but France played a great role in the development of his musical genius." Then you began to praise France, declaring that France is the one nation capable of embracing Arabic culture, not only because of the presence of large numbers of Arab immigrants there, but because the French sensibility is so close to the Arab one: namely, their love of for life and art. "You have a rosy view of French society," Lucine replies. "It's a nation of people that feel no wonder about anything: the people are always blasé and critical—even of themselves. The French have changed a lot from the days when al-Tahtawi and Taha Hussein wrote about France." Then she excuses herself to take a bath. You step out onto the balcony and look down on Talaat Harb Street from high up. It seems like a magical world, and you wish someone would take your picture with this magical scene in the background, the way world-famous actors do, especially the image imprinted in your brain of Marilyn Monroe and James Dean as they look down in contemplation and sadness over New York City on a day when fog fills the balcony. Tiny cars can be seen, with storefronts extending in both directions, as people amble along, looking like ants. You remember *Gulliver's Travels*, and homes and buildings in the French style, the kind that Khedive Ismail dreamed of. You dream of living downtown one day like all artists in the world do, where the museums, cinema, opera, bookstores, and life are. But you always return to Maadi, as if fate is forcing you to live there with people you don't enjoy being with very much. You don't understand what they want out of life, other than a luxury car and a fancy apartment. Even your friends are different from you: they are blown away by Sadat and his national project, and forget all about Nasser. They think of Nasser as the big fool that got the region entangled in wars we were incapable of winning; that he was the one who ushered into the region the modern colonialism of America and Israel, after he nationalized the Suez Canal—which Egypt would have gotten back anyway a few years after 1956.

After that you will find out that Lucine left Cairo, not only because she had finished her year of studies at Cairo University's Egyptology department, but also to return to Paris to have her baby, since she had misgivings about giving birth in Cairo. You stop hearing news about her, and some time later, you meet up with Basim and go with him to his apartment. He brings you out onto the balcony and takes some photos out of his pocket. "These are pictures of my son Shihab with that French woman Lucine," he tells you. You have no idea whether to believe him or not. You stare at the photos and see the striking resemblance between father and son, then you ask him, "Will Lucine ever come back to Cairo?" He looks out at the vast desert in the distance and sighs. "That whore told me, 'If you want to see him, you have to come to France.' She knows for certain that that's impossible. As you know, I don't have a passport. She claims she doesn't have the money."

"Maybe she's afraid that if she comes, you'll take the child from her," you say.

"Really? Maybe . . . ." Then he is silent for a little, and says, "I want someone who can take care of me, but she's just a fantasy. I'm not such a jerk that I would deprive a child of his mother: he needs her more than me."

"What's his religion?" I ask.

"That's a good question. She's a Christian, of course. She's a strict Catholic, even though she believed in Islam. She used to read the Qur'an a lot, and it wasn't just for her class requirements: she liked getting to know the Book, which transformed villagers living in Mecca, and then Medina, into an umma that rules whole peoples, and that creates civilizations that have been the talk of the world, and that were a source of knowledge for many nations." Then he added that her father was a deacon in a church somewhere in France, and that he had lived for a time in Lebanon, and Egypt, too. "When Lucine told him about my numerous past relationships, he told her that in Islam, a Muslim is allowed to enjoy women however he wishes to, under what is called 'What the Right Hand Possesses.' So you're now the possession of his right hand, he told her, so enjoy it. Despite her sin with me, she loves the Messiah and considers him to be the ideal example to believe in. She believes he will help her be rid of me. The child's religion isn't the important thing. The important thing is that he knows who his father is, and grows up believing in the one God, believing that this world has a Creator, and that nature didn't create itself. Maybe he will grow up believing in the existentialism that Sartre and Camus called for," he added with a sigh. "The struggle between nonexistence and existence—those are the two things that intimidate France."

You will often see him sitting for hours in the al-Hurreya Coffeehouse on Bab al-Luq Square as he watches the chess players and is absorbed in cracking jokes with them. Then he begins playing with them for hours, late into the night, until his spine creaks from sitting so long in one position. He will tell you that no one will ever beat him, not in this coffeeshop, not even in the whole world. He will be the fastest player to move pieces on the board and reset the timer. You will ask him why he doesn't play the game professionally, since he's so skilled at it. The important thing is that you succeed at something, and he will tell you, "Your problem is that you believe that everything you do has to turn a profit. For example, you write stories and novels and don't make any profit off them, except a few sentences of praise. Not many people read your books. You will live more than thirty years until anyone acknowledges you, and maybe you'll be dead by then, and no one will give you a prize to make that the crowning achievement of your efforts."

Nadir, you will go too, to the al-Hurreya Coffeehouse, to sit among people and try to understand why they are sitting that way. You began with curiosity, then you became addicted to sitting among them, incapable of throwing yourself into it, and utterly failing to learn the game of chess, in spite of your friend Hazim's attempts to teach you. You see young Milad, the coffeeshop waiter, joking with the foreigners and whispering sexual innuendos. He circumspectly feels up women's backs and intimidates the men by sitting on the women's laps, and they are astonished by his boldness.

Shyly, you sit in the area where alcoholic drinks aren't served, fleeing any table where you happen to find a bottle of Stella beer, afraid that one of your friends or acquaintances might see you and suspect you of being dissolute, or so you imagine.

❖

Basim will tell you, "You should discover Egypt," and he will invite you on a safari trip to the western oases. He will tell you that the Sahara will help you write, and create a desert atmosphere for your novel; that foreigners understand Egypt's beauty in all its senses; that the white mountains and warm sands will restore your clarity of mind to you; that nature is the best teacher.

He will say, "You have to get out of Maadi: it's an utterly uninspiring neighborhood. The only people who live there are a group of bourgeois who are looking for the quiet life without taking risks or experiencing anything." He will take you in his small car and reveal Wadi Digla to you. He will show you some fossilized whale bones from millions of years ago, and lead you via new shortcuts that take you from Maadi to Nasr City in a matter of minutes, cutting across the desert, zigzagging paths, and cemeteries.

He will advise you that it is up to the writer to liberate himself from a monotonous life and live so that he can set his imagination free, and to get to know strangers, because they are capable of helping you do that; because they astonish you with the ingenuousness of their stories and their oddness, and their intense love of life. The world is the paradise that they created for its own sake; they work and struggle to create it. Thus, you see their love for life, and their intense desire to enjoy every moment of it. Today is history, and the future is something held in safekeeping for the joy of the lived moment.

❖

As he walked the crowded city streets, Nadir looked at the numerous shops. On the left was the BTM store displaying winter coats. He stared at them, then entered the establishment. "I'll buy a coat this winter," he said. "They're predicting it will be biting cold. I'll buy a pair of gloves to protect my fingers from frostbite. Maybe I'll also get myself a hat. I won't be accused of what people say about me, that I'm trying to imitate western men." Then he whispered to himself, as he tries on the coat, "I'll live by myself. I'll rent an apartment— it should look out over a main street and a wide-open space. I'll buy a comfortable new American-style couch, and a desk and an armchair, and Beethoven recordings, and the *Red Lips* album by Muhammad Mounir. I'll try not to feel guilty about the decisions I've made, especially about divorcing my wife. I will try to begin again—the beginnings of things are so beautiful! Maybe I will achieve happiness for myself. Maybe!"

❖

You will see Basim standing in front of the Nasserist Party building, shouting out with many of his fellow citizens as they demand free and fair elections. Their chanting is mixed with the voice of Nancy Agram as she sings, "I Can't Take You . . . I Can't Leave You." You ask yourself, "Will Nancy retire from singing when America leaves Iraq, or not?" You laugh when you hear young guys, the kind that use large amounts of hair gel and wear strange clothes (proving that globalization has

194

succeeded in Egypt), laughing at the demonstrators. You head their way and approach them, and urge them to stay away from this place, since the police and Central Security have it surrounded. It's possible that violence will flare up between the people and the police.

You leave them shouting along with the masses and you set off. Then you hear nothing but gunshots, and see only clouds of smoke.

Cairo–Dublin–Paris–Cairo
(1993–2001)

Glossary

Abd al-Halim Hafez (1929–77) iconic Egyptian singer and actor, wildly popular throughout the Arab world in the 1960s and 1970s. Known as "the Dark Nightingale," his music was associated with the Arab nationalism of the period.

Ahmad Shawqi (1868–1932) major Egyptian poet of the early twentieth century. His "Prophet's Hamza" is a poem in praise of the Prophet Muhammad.

Al-Azhar name for both a historic Cairo mosque and its attached university, one of the most important cultural centers of religious scholarship in Sunni Islam.

Allahu Akbar! God is great!

Antique-Khana Museum a predecessor of Cairo's Museum of Islamic Art. Housed in what was then Egypt's National Library, it featured antiquities from Egypt's Islamic period.

Bahr al-Baqar an Egyptian village near the Suez Canal, site of a 1970 Israeli air raid that killed forty-six schoolchildren.

Baligh Hamdi (1932–93) a popular Egyptian composer who wrote songs for a number of Egyptian singers, including Umm Kulthum and Abd al-Halim Hafez.

Batniya a working-class neighborhood in the Darb al-Ahmar district of Cairo, notorious for drug dealers and gangs.

". . . believed in their Lord, and We increased them in guidance" from the Qur'an, 18:13 (Surat al-Kahf).

Café Riche popular Cairo café frequented by Egyptian literati and artists.

"Eggs, lettuce, and salted fish" foods associated with the popular Egyptian holiday of Shamm al-Nessim (Sniffing the Breeze), which marks the arrival of spring.

". . . erase the cross from his wrist" many Copts, as a symbol of their piety and religious identity, have a cross tattooed on their right wrist.

Fairuz (b. 1932) a beloved Lebanese chanteuse whose songs are familiar across the Arab world.

Fathy Abdalla and Hassan Khadr are Egyptian poets who came of age in the 1980s and are known for writing prose poetry *(qasidat al-nathr)*.

fuul broad beans. A staple of Egyptian cooking.

Hamdin Sabbahi a leftist political reformer and founder of Egypt's socialist/Nasserist al-Karama (Dignity) Party.

Hasan al-Banna (1906–49) founder of Egypt's Muslim Brotherhood.

"He created the heavens and the earth in six days and then sat upon the Throne." From the Qur'an 10:3 (Surat Yunus).

"He who has given you the Qur'an will surely bring you back to the place of return." From the Qur'an, 28:85 (Surat al-Qasas).

Helwan an industrial district south of Cairo.

"If someone takes your cloak, do not stop him from taking your tunic." From Luke 6:29 of the New Testament (New International Version translation).

Imbaba a crowded working-class district in Cairo, on the west side of the Nile.

Insha'allah Arabic for "God willing," widely used in everyday conversation.

"Inta Umri" one of the most popular songs performed by the Egyptian singer Umm Kulthum.

jilbab a long, loose-fitting garment.

khawaga general term used to refer to a non-Egyptian of European background.

Khedive Ismail (1830–95) a grandson of Muhammad Ali Pasha who ruled Egypt as Khedive from 1863 to 1879. His era is associated with lavish spending, the inauguration of the Suez Canal, and construction projects that introduced nineteenth-century European architecture to downtown Cairo.

kushari quintessential Egyptian street food: a filling dish of noodles, rice, lentils, and chickpeas, topped with a vinegary tomato sauce and fried onions.

Lake Qarun a large salty lake on the north side of the Fayoum depression, located southwest of Cairo. According to local legend, it takes its name from an evil ruler of the Fayoum who was divinely punished for his arrogance by drowning in the lake.

Maadi a leafy, upscale Cairo residential district to the south of the city center.

maazun an official who registers Muslim marriages.

Midian a city, mentioned several times in the Qur'an, to which Moses fled after killing a man in Egypt. See Qur'an, Sura 28 (al-Qasas), v. 21–23.

Mosque of 'Amr ibn al-'As the oldest mosque in Africa, located near Old Cairo. The mosque was built by (and named for) the Arab military commander who conquered Egypt for Islam in AD 641. Its numerous alterations and restorations over the centuries mean that very little of its original architecture is left.

Mugamma a massive government building on Cairo's Tahrir Square, filled with a maze of offices. A symbol of complex government bureaucracy.

Muhammad Hasanein Heikal (b. 1923) leading Egyptian journalist and close confidante of President Gamal Abd al-Nasser.

mulid festival commemorating the birthdate of a saint or other religious figure, whether Muslim or Christian. Mulids often take the form of lively street festivals.

Mustafa Kamil (1874–1908) prominent Egyptian nationalist leader during the period of British occupation.

Naksa Arabic for 'setback' or 'debacle.' Commonly used to refer to the defeat of Arab forces in the June War of 1967.

Nasr City an upscale neighborhood east of downtown Cairo, built during the 1960s. President Sadat was assassinated there in 1981 during an annual military parade.

qanun a stringed instrument resembling a zither or dulcimer.

Qarun's Palace a well-preserved Greco-Roman temple filled with dark corridors and chambers that sits south of Lake Qarun.

ratl a standard measure of weight, equal to about half a kilogram.

Romantica a bittersweet 1996 Egyptian film about a group of illegal tour guides who befriend tourists in Cairo.

Safiya Zaghloul wife of early twentieth-century nationalist hero Saad Zaghloul. A street in Alexandria is named after her.

Shaykh Imam (1918–95) a blind Egyptian singer and composer who formed one half of a popular duo with poet and singer Ahmad Fuad Negm. Their political songs often had a left-wing, populist bent, and were highly critical of the Egyptian government after the 1967 War.

Sidi Ibn al-Farid an early-thirteenth-century Egyptian poet and Sufi mystic, known for his ecstatic visions. His tomb is located near the Muqattam Hills east of Cairo, and his *mulid* is celebrated with a two-day festival where his poems are set to music and performed.

sirwal traditional loose-fitting trousers, usually held up by a drawstring.

takfir among modern Islamic fundamentalists, an accusation of apostasy. Specifically, a declaration that other Muslims (or Muslim societies) have strayed so far from Islam that they should be considered unbelievers.

Umm Hashim another name for Sayyida Zaynab (d. 680), a granddaughter of the Prophet Muhammad, whose mosque in downtown Cairo has long been a popular focus of devotion for Egyptian Muslims.

urfi literally, 'customary.' Refers to the practice of informal or temporary marriage considered by many to be acceptable in Islam.

Wadi Digla a natural protectorate not far from the Maadi district, south of Cairo, popular with hikers and known for its petrified wood, rock formations, and fossils.

Zamalek a leafy, upper-class neighborhood on an island near downtown Cairo.

zikr literally a 'remembrance of God,' a Sufi ritual in which adherents recite God's name repeatedly, often while moving rhythmically.

Modern Arabic Literature
from the American University in Cairo Press